"Two months from the engagement we'll be married!"

Roslyn felt a frisson of panic, then a great curl of rapture. "How am I going to organize a big wedding in *that* time?"

"I honestly don't know. You *want* a big wedding?"

"Yes, I do!" Her voice shook a little.

"You'll make an unforgettable bride!" His eyes swept over her, amazingly sensual, amazingly blue.

"It's a fantasy, isn't it?" Even now she was experiencing a sensation like dreaming.

"More, it's a marriage!" Marsh answered almost tautly.

Dear Reader,

Harlequin Romance would like to welcome you
Back To The Ranch again with our year long miniseries
Hitched! We've rounded up twelve of our most popular
authors, and the result is a whole year of romance,
Western-style: cool cowboys, rugged ranchers and,
of course, the women who tame them.

The trail starts with Margaret Way and *A Faulkner
Possession* (#3391). Roslyn thought she'd put the
past and her youthful infatuation with rancher
Marsh Faulkner behind her. But Marsh wanted a
"trophy" wife, and Roslyn fitted the bill—love
didn't enter into it. Though Roslyn was tempted,
she couldn't reconcile herself to being just another
Faulkner possession.

Next month Renee Roszel will be heading West with a
Valentine story, *To Lasso a Lady* (#3397). Some cowboys
think they know it all—and how can a girl resist
proving them wrong?

Look out for books branded Hitched! in the coming
months. We'll be featuring books by all your favorite
names: Patricia Knoll, Ruth Jean Dale, Rebecca Winters
and Patricia Wilson, to mention a few!

Happy reading!

The Editors
Harlequin Romance

How the West was wooed!

A Faulkner Possession
Margaret Way

Harlequin Books

TORONTO • NEW YORK • LONDON
AMSTERDAM • PARIS • SYDNEY • HAMBURG
STOCKHOLM • ATHENS • TOKYO • MILAN
MADRID • WARSAW • BUDAPEST • AUCKLAND

ISBN 0-373-03391-5

A FAULKNER POSSESSION

First North American Publication 1996.

CHAPTER ONE

END of school. It invoked so many memories, exquisite and painful, time was suspended while Roslyn became lost in them. Students and fellow teachers were mostly long gone, but she continued to sit at her desk staring out broodingly over the beautifully manicured lawns and gardens of Seymour College for Girls. There were many jacarandas in bloom in the grounds, but instead of emerald sweeps of lawn and a glorious, lavender blue haze, her inner eye was possessed by her old visions....

The immensity of the desert...a burning sun going down over infinite miles of red sand...towering, windswept dunes transformed by the sunset into pyramids of gold...a raven-haired young man—how beautiful he was astride a wonderful, palomino horse—a small girl up before him, her enormous topaz eyes full of wonder and adoration for all the vast chasm between them.

Macumba. Marsh Faulkner. It gave her no peace to think of them. Marsh, once her idol, now the man she struggled daily to keep from her thoughts. The old, remarkable friendship? Banished without a trace. Except for memories. Memories had the power to return at any time, like old passions that refused to die.

Roslyn's eyes clouded with melancholy. She slumped back in her chair unaware her hands were gripping the mahogany arms. It wasn't as though she hadn't tried. Even now she blinked furiously in an effort to dispel those haunting images, but they continued to possess

5

her; so vivid, so immediate, she felt nostalgia and pain in every cell of her heart.

For most of her childhood and adolescence, the end of term meant only one thing. The return to Macumba. Stronghold of the Faulkners. Flagship of Faulkner Holdings, a beef cattle empire that spread its operations over the giant state of Queensland, from its desert heartland to the lush jungles of the tropic north and into the vast wilderness of the Northern Territory, one of the world's last great frontiers. The Faulkners, descendants of the founding fathers, were the landed establishment, enormously rich and powerful, and heirs to a splendid, historic homestead that had in its history entertained royalty, Indian maharajahs and countless VIP's.

And my mother is the housekeeper, Roslyn thought. The whole thing just broke her to pieces. Her beautiful, hardworking, incredibly loyal and long-suffering mother was housekeeper to the Faulkners and had been for the past ten years. She would never come to terms with it, her nature behind the cool facade, bright, passionate and above all, proud. My mother, all I have in this world, is just another Faulkner possession. She could be here with me, free and independent, yet she chooses to remain in service. It didn't bear thinking about, and most of the time Roslyn couldn't. Her great purpose in life since she'd been able to earn money was to provide for her mother: to repay all her mother's endless sacrifices. She had a house: there was room: they could live together. Except for the grievous fact her mother chose to remain on Macumba.

Oh, hell!

Roslyn stood up so precipitously she sent a pile of textbooks on the edge of her desk flying. Sighing, she bent to retrieve them and as she did so, Dave Arnold, the junior science master came into the room. He took one look at her and hurried around the desk.

"Here, let me get those, Ros!"

This was the colleague who had lit up Dave's year. Roslyn Earnshaw. A slender, graceful young woman, average height, great legs, slight but sensual curves, wonderful dark hair he had sometimes seen in a cloud, now neatly confined at the nape; large, faintly slanted topaz eyes, a flawless magnolia skin that was the envy of all Seymour. Dave, like everyone else, thought Roslyn a natural beauty who played down her looks. She was always beautifully groomed in good, classic clothes, but Dave thought quite another person lurked behind the contained exterior. A witching, passionate person with a volatility just below the surface. Not that her pupils didn't love her. They adored her like an older, more beautiful and clever sister. But then, Roslyn showed another side to her students. It was with staff that she maintained a pleasant, but impenetrable reserve. She was highly regarded as a teacher, but no one knew much about her private life. Roslyn Earnshaw was something of an enigma, which greatly endeared her to Dave who found mysterious young women terribly glamorous.

He stacked the books on the desk and Roslyn thanked him with a smile. Sadness to sunshine! It entranced Dave, who asked, as if he didn't already know, "Your car is being serviced, isn't it?"

Roslyn pulled down the window and locked it. "Don't worry about me, Dave. I thought you long gone."

"Without saying goodbye?"

She looked at him with gentle wryness. "You *did* say goodbye. At the staff party."

"That was public. This is private. Besides, someone has to drive you home."

"You do have a kind heart, Dave. Thank you. I'm very grateful."

A few minutes later they were walking through the empty corridors and out to the staff parking lot, its functionalism masked by tall borders of flowering oleanders. Seymour was justifiably proud of its magnificent grounds. The annual Spring garden party drew huge crowds.

"What do you intend to do with yourself over the holidays?" Dave asked as they were driving away.

"I haven't decided yet." Roslyn gave a faint sigh. "My mother wants me to visit her, but there are complications."

"Such as?" Dave was curious.

"Other people, Dave. Other people to spoil things."

Dave took a moment to digest that. "I see." He glanced at her quickly. "You never talk much about your family. In fact, you never talk about them at all."

"I haven't got much of a family, that's why. I'm an only child. My father was killed when I was fourteen."

"I'm sorry, Roslyn," Dave said with genuine sympathy. "That accounts for the sad look."

"I didn't know I had one."

"You do. The reverse of the super-efficient look we all know. But getting back to your mother, has she remarried? Is that it?"

She should have remarried. She should have had someone to love her, Roslyn thought. "Mother never remarried," she told Dave. "My father was something of an adventurer. As a young man he packed a bag and headed for the outback to become a jackaroo. He thrived on station life, tough as it is. Eventually he got to manage an outstation. When he was twenty-six he met my mother. She was an English girl working her way around

Australia with a friend. Her mother died when she was three. Her father remarried a year later and started another family. According to my mother, her stepmother never wanted her and things got worse as my mother grew up. I should tell you, she's beautiful, and that doesn't always make for a happy life. Her upbringing made her very vulnerable. Sometimes I think she's still a lost child.

"Anyway, she left home as soon as she was able and came to Australia with her friend, Ruth. They've kept in touch through the years. My father fell in love with my mother at first sight. He could never get over the wonder of getting her to marry him, he said. She was so refined and gently spoken and he was very much the prototype of Crocodile Dundee, funny, gritty, very direct. I loved him and he adored his two girls. Once he was settled, he started stepping up the ladder. When I was about ten, he became head stockman of a very grand station indeed. Life was a lot easier and settled for my mother. A nice bungalow, more money, permanency if things worked out. They did. Dad did become overseer, but he was killed a little over a year later."

Dave took his eyes off the road to stare at her. "How did it happen?"

"He was thrown from his horse and broke his neck. He had lived in the saddle, that was the tragic irony. My mother never got over it. For me the pain has dulled with the years, but I've always been conscious of *loss*, of missing him. An expression, a song, the scent of the bush makes it all come rushing back. Life is so *sad*!"

"It is for a lot of people. Where is your mother now?"

"Still at the same place." Roslyn couldn't control the strain in her voice. "After Dad was killed, the owner offered her a job and she took it."

"You don't sound too happy about it?"

"Not then and not now," Roslyn admitted. "We could have made it on our own."

"But you said yourself your mother is a vulnerable woman. She would have been devastated at the time. Widowed so early with a young daughter. Times like that, people either make a complete break or stick with what they know. What job was it?"

"Housekeeper," Roslyn announced flatly.

"So?" Dave turned his head in surprise. "You're not a snob, are you?"

"I am and you'd better believe it! Where my *mother* is concerned. I can't bear to see her at anyone's beck and call. Especially not them. I worked like a demon all through school and university. I graduated in the top three of my class. Seymour took me on and they don't take just anybody, as you know. I make good money and I can look after my mother." There I go again, she thought. A fixation. I can't leave the subject alone.

"Are you quite sure she can't look after herself?" Dave asked as gently as he could.

Roslyn closed her eyes. "Oh, Dave, you *can't* know. One has to experience what I'm talking about. These people are enormously rich and powerful. They aren't like you and me. They say the rich are different. They *are*. They have super and often unwarranted confidence in themselves and their opinions. They move through life like the lords of creation. Some of the women can be unbearable. I've known a few who were affronted I would dare speak to them. Others found me quaint. Some women like throwing their menfolk's power around." She gave a little embarrassed laugh. "I know I sound like I've got a giant chip on my shoulder. I have. But I grew up a kid people could, and did, hurt."

"Well, it doesn't show," Dave said comfortingly. "Hardly a girl in the school doesn't dream of looking and sounding like Miss Earnshaw."

Roslyn shook her head, smiling slightly. "It's my skin they like, Dave. Spots can make the teen years a torment. Don't think too badly of me. It's just that I want a better life for my mother."

"It hurts she won't come and live with you?"

"It does. Rather badly. It's all I've worked for, but she says I must be free to live my own life. She's content where she is."

"So why don't you accept it?"

Roslyn shrugged. "You wouldn't, either, Dave. This isn't a nice family situation like the Brady Bunch. Anyway, I don't believe her. My mother is only fifty years old. She's a beautiful woman but she's had such a hard life. At least, not one of her own. Think what other women are doing at her age. She hasn't really lived at all."

There was a short pause while Dave considered. "I can see your point, Ros," he said finally, "but it's *your* point, isn't it? Your mother's tragedies may have robbed her of a lot of fight. So, what is this place we're talking about? You're terribly secretive."

Roslyn glanced down at her locked hands. "I suppose I am. I like to keep my private life private, but end of term depletes my reserves. I start harking back to the old days. Always a mistake. They're there waiting for me if I let down my guard. I've told you more than I've told most people. The name of the station is Macumba. Macumba Downs."

Dave looked flabbergasted. "But that's the *Faulkner* place!"

"Snap out of it, Dave. They're human."

"They're *not*! Why, the old guy—the founding father—is an icon. I'll be honest with you, Ros, I'm amazed. Wasn't a Faulkner killed in a plane crash a few years ago?"

"Sir Charles, the owner," Roslyn said, her expression turning sad. "His plane came down in a freak electrical storm en route to one of their northern properties. Sir Charles and Lady Faulkner were killed, along with two passengers. One was a lifelong American friend. The other was Sir Charles's younger brother, Hugo." She didn't say Marsh had been scheduled to go with them but some crisis had kept him on the station. She often had nightmares about Marsh dying in that crash.

Dave was engrossed. "What a tragedy!" he breathed. "It must have been the son on television recently. Something to do with beef cattle exports to Japan and South-East Asia. I haven't a lot of interest in the subject, but he made me sit up and take notice. Electrifying kind of guy. Founding family. Old money. Doesn't have to prove anything. Is he married? Bound to be."

Roslyn shook her head. "No, he isn't."

"He must be the biggest catch in the country!" Dave chortled.

"He knows it."

"I imagine he might. His name is Charles, too, as I recall."

Roslyn looked out the window. "Everyone calls him Marsh. Marshall is his middle name. It was Lady Faulkner's maiden name. The Marshalls still control the Mossvale Pastoral Company."

Dave made another little howling sound. "Mossvale! Gosh, isn't it always the way. Money marries money."

"It keeps it all together."

"And how do you feel about Marsh Faulkner?" Dave asked. "He seems like the kind of guy to arouse powerful feelings."

Roslyn smoothed her skirt over her knee. "He is."

Dave was intrigued by the thread of steel in Roslyn's attractive, low-pitched voice. "Can you elaborate on that?"

"Not a chance! Let's get off the subject, Dave."

"It does have a disturbing ring," he agreed.

Ten minutes later they turned onto Roslyn's quiet, tree-lined street made a glory by the summer flowering of the poincianas. Dave commented on their spectacular beauty as they drove past the comfortable, modern homes until he came to Roslyn's low-set house. Once the most ordinary house on the street, she had transformed it with a stylish brick and wrought-iron fence and a re-planted garden.

"I'll bring the carton of books in, shall I?" Dave asked hopefully.

There was absolutely no point in encouraging him. "Thanks, Dave, but it's not heavy," Roslyn said gently.

"Then I'll be off!" Dave answered breezily, covering up his disappointment. "Take care, Ros. Enjoy your holidays." He bent quickly, kissed her cheek, then lopped back to his car.

Roslyn stood at the front gate, waving him off. Dave was nice. A pleasant companion on several occasions this past year. What did she want? Another bolt of lightning?

There was mail and she skimmed through it. Her head was aching from too much talk about Macumba. She unfastened the clip at her nape, shaking her dark cloud of hair free. Ah, that was better! She always thought of her prim knot as a form of disguise.

The gardenia bushes she had planted in a shady corner of the garden were smothered in blossom. She veered off to pick one, twirling it appreciatively beneath her nose. If only camellias had this wonderful scent! When she had changed her clothes, she would turn the sprinklers on. She loved her garden. Everything she had planted was thriving thanks to all her hard work. It was hard to believe she had her own home even if it would take her a lot of years to pay it off.

Her mother had wanted her to buy a home unit, thinking she would be more secure, but Roslyn, reared to the vast, open spaces, couldn't bear the thought of being cooped up. Besides, she loved a garden and she had to have somewhere for her piano. An accomplished pianist, the piano, a baby grand, had been her mother's twenty-first birthday present to her. Roslyn treasured it, even if it never ceased to bother her that her mother had spent so much of her savings on it. Yet, wasn't it part of the pattern? Her parents had lavished their last penny on her. She had gone to an excellent boarding school from age ten to seventeen. A straight-A student, her mother had insisted she go on to university, which was what Roslyn desperately wanted but had accepted as out of the question. Where was the money to come from?

Somehow, between the two of them, they had managed. Roslyn had worked her way through university, waitressing in a friend's mother's restaurant and tutoring at a coaching college; an exhausting grind with all her assignments, but she was young, eager, and she had a goal. To look after her mother. She had gone straight from university to Seymour, a top-rated private school for girls. She considered herself one of the lucky ones. She had several good friends from her university days and as much social life as she wanted. So why did she feel so empty, so unfulfilled? Teaching wasn't enough, though it did give her a sense of satisfaction and purpose.

The great sadness of her life was that her mother had chosen the Faulkners over her. She had endured all those years under Lady Faulkner. Dreadful to speak ill of the dead, but Lady Faulkner had been an unbearable woman. Imperious, brook-no-nonsense, full of demands that were never properly met. Roslyn had a stark vision of herself as a child sprawling in the dust because Lady Faulkner had struck her with a riding crop.

She could see Lady Faulkner now, her strong, high-boned features too severe for beauty, but handsome, as a lioness is handsome, tawny-haired, ice-blue eyes, freckled, weathered skin, in her riding boots, six feet tall. A terrifying sight to a child, yet Roslyn had shouted up at her, "You horrible, nasty woman! I did not frighten Rajah!"

A stockman's child to dare answer back the mistress of Macumba and in such a fashion! Sir Charles coming on them, had broken up the incident, shocked and stern. Marsh had raced to her, picked her up and brushed her down. From that day he had placed himself between Roslyn and his mother. A state of affairs that had continued right up until Lady Faulkner's death. Lady Faulkner had never struck her again, but there had been barbs galore and a chilling condescension. The whole outback had mourned Sir Charles's death. Lady Faulkner's passing had elicited private sighs of relief. Sybill Faulkner had always been deferred to in her lifetime, but never liked. All the warmth in her had been reserved for her only son. Even her daughters had understood they could not compete with Marsh for their mother's love and attention. Yet both of them had inherited her height, her tawny colouring and autocratic ways. The Marshall Inheritance, most people called it. It had made Macumba no place for Roslyn and a difficult one for her mother. Yet her mother had stayed. Why? What had been the hold? Mostly Roslyn closed her eyes to it as though investigation would only open a Pandora's box.

Lost in her reflections Roslyn was almost at the short flight of steps that led to the veranda, when her heart gave a great, warning leap. A man who had been sitting in one of the wicker chairs suddenly rose to his feet, giving Roslyn a glimpse of a tall, rangy figure in elegant, city clothes.

Yet hadn't she been expecting it?

He moved along the veranda with indolent grace, out of the cool, golden-green shadows into the full sunlight, a saturnine expression on his marvellous face.

Marsh. A man no woman could forget. Certainly not Roslyn.

The old, dark excitement struck. *"You!"* She was aware, as always, of the magnetism that passed between them.

"Me. Sweet Rosa!" His dazzling, bluer than blue eyes moved over her as if reminding her they knew every inch of her and she'd been his for the taking.

"What are you doing here?" she asked in her coolest tone.

"Never mind that. What do you think you're doing with another man?"

"I'm a free agent, Marsh. Just like you."

"Fine words, Rosa. Come closer." Blue eyes narrowed and a taunting smile played around the beautiful, sardonic mouth.

"Thank you, Marsh." She shrugged. "This *is* my house." Studiously casual, she tossed the gardenia into the shrubbery and walked quickly up the steps. Into, as she thought, the lion's den. Her whole body was warming as the dark flames moved through her and she hoped the telltale colour wasn't showing in her cheeks.

"And very nice it is, too," Marsh was saying in a mock conciliatory voice. "I love the garden. All your work? I was thinking maybe a small sculpture?"

Her dark cloud of hair flew around her face as her quick temper sizzled. "Don't start patronising me. I can't stand that."

"Goodness, no!" he answered, and there was an infuriating little hint of laughter in the vibrant tones. "It's like waving a red flag in front of a bull. Settle down, poppet. I haven't seen you in months. The last time a bare ten minutes at your school and you were *freezing*!"

"What were you expecting? A dazzling display of affection?"

"Easy enough in the old days," he reminded her with more than a touch of cruelty.

The days when he had total dominion over her. Roslyn flushed. "I stopped caring about you a long time ago."

He only smiled at her, his teeth a flash of white against a dark tan. "I'll live with it, Rosa. So why are *you* so miserable?"

Roslyn touched a quick hand to her forehead. It seemed to be burning. "That's the whole point, Marsh. I'm not. The only thing that bugs me is not having Mother."

"Her choice, Rosa. Don't keep blaming me. Liv's not like you. Life has sobered her. She's not determined and headstrong, like you. She's a gentle, retiring person. Not an argumentative, prickly little fire-eater. Liv feels safe at Macumba."

"More like you have some hold on her, like your father before you!" Roslyn blurted, wanting to strike him physically she was so angry at his easy, instant effect on her. "And who said you could call her Liv?"

"She likes it," he snapped. "I'm the new regime, Roslyn. You can't seem to get that into your head. Now, I'd like to go into the house, if you don't mind. One of your neighbours has been eyeing me suspiciously for the past fifteen minutes."

"That's no surprise! Most women give you open-mouthed attention." Roslyn moved down along the veranda. "It's a wonder you didn't find the key."

"As a matter of fact, I did. Casually pushed down the side of that basket of orchids you're making for. Not a good idea, poppet. A beautiful young woman living alone can't be too careful."

"Who said I was living alone?" The key retrieved, she swept past him, her every movement as mettlesome as a high-stepping filly.

"*Aren't* you?" Without appearing to move, he had her by the arm. A touch that weakened her knees and brought back a terrifying leap of rapture.

"Take your hands off me, Marsh," she managed with commendable calm. "What I do is none of your business."

The mesmeric gaze sharpened into irony. "After all these years? Face it, Rosa. I'm always going to keep an eye on you."

"You'll get tired of it." Cold reason demanded she pull away. "What are you really in town for? I'm sure it's not to see me."

"Come on," he lightly jeered. "Would I pass up the chance? It so happens I'm meeting up with a few of my colleagues. Business and pleasure. Liv explained your reluctance to come to us."

"I think I put it with more vigour." Roslyn inserted the key in the lock. "The truth is, Marsh, I've had enough of you and your precious Macumba to last me a lifetime."

"You don't mean that." He followed her in. "What's regressive about you is, you keep harking back to the past. You're not the only one who felt pain."

Inside the quiet house his presence was doubly disturbing. "So you admit it? There *was* pain?" Her question was a challenge.

"Of course I admit it. Stop working yourself up. You always were too damned sensitive to everything. Offer me a cup of coffee before I'm forced to make it myself."

"When did you ever make yourself anything?" she flared.

He stared at her so she felt the full weight of his natural authority. "Are you trying to tell me I don't do a day's work?"

"All right, so I put that unfairly." Roslyn shook her head as though to clear it of little demons. "I know how hard you work, Marsh. Incredibly hard. I only meant you get waited on, as well."

"Rosa, you're a worse snob than any of us. I consider having a housekeeper to prepare my meals perfectly normal. For one thing, I don't have the time or inclination and it gives someone a job. You've always taken the view your mother was sold into slavery. We've always had household staff. Is that a sin? We can afford it and the homestead is huge. I can't think of anyone who would care to run it on their own. All in all, we have hundreds of employees. None of them forced to stay. Most of them I would think, happy enough. And that includes Liv. She takes great pride in her efficiency."

"In fact, she's had an awful time and you know that perfectly well," Roslyn said in a tight voice. "When my father was killed she was too bereft to think for herself. I wasn't old enough to be much use. I bitterly regret that. Your father offered her the job and not even your mother would go against him but she never liked us."

"My mother never liked anyone," Marsh answered with bleak humour.

"Except *you*. She adored you. You were the only person in her life. I used to feel so sorry for your sisters. Anyone else but your mother would have been besotted with Sir Charles."

Marsh gave a harsh sigh. "My parents' marriage wasn't a love match. You know that. They were paired off almost from the day they were born. It's not all that unusual. Everyone thought it would work. It didn't. My mother and father led separate lives but they elected to stay under one roof. My father didn't believe in divorce. He'd made his commitment and that was that. You know what he was like."

Roslyn lowered her head, feeling a quiver of shame. "An honorable man but not a happy one. Like you, he was laden with too many responsibilities. Too much expectation. Old school. Old values. Isn't it better to split up than live a lie?"

Marsh gave her a hard, impatient glance. "And what about the children, family, the continuity of tradition? There are worse things than staying together. Like pulling everyone apart. All we have to do, Roslyn, is solve our own problems. Not everyone else's. Not even your mother's. People don't always do what we want. My father had powerful reasons for doing all the things he did. That's good enough for me.''

"Well, it's not good enough for me!" Roslyn announced dramatically. "Sir Charles blackmailed my mother into staying."

Inflammatory words! Goaded, Marsh grasped her by the shoulders. "So he cared about what happened to her? There was no relationship, if that's what you're implying."

So profoundly protective of her mother, Roslyn decided to take affront. "Dear me, no!" she cried. "How could such a thing happen? The exalted Sir Charles Faulkner, pillar of the establishment, a genuine gentleman, and his housekeeper? We're talking sacrilege here!"

The blue eyes blazed. Blue. Blue, bluer. "Don't say another word, Roslyn," he growled.

It was insanity to ignore him. "You're hurting me," she said, looking pointedly at his hands.

"I'm sorry." Abruptly he released her. With a characteristic upthrust of his head he walked away down the hallway with its polished floor and bright Indian runner, glancing left and right before turning into the kitchen at the rear of the house.

Roslyn stood for a moment, trying to cool down. The last time they had been together their meeting had ended in bitter argument. Mostly her fault. She acknowledged her guilts, but she had received too many painful blows from Faulkner hands.

When she walked into the kitchen, Marsh was looking moodily around. Roslyn was rather proud of the way she had transformed the kitchen with sunshine yellow paint and a glossy white trim. Filmy white curtains adorned the windows, a circular pine table and chairs occupied the center of the room, an old pine dresser she used to display a very pretty Victorian dinner set against the wall. A mixed bunch of flowers stood on the table, another at the window behind the sink. Everything was spick-and-span as was her way. Her mother had trained her well.

Not that she expected Marsh to notice. He was used to grandeur. He had known it from the cot. Her first cot had been a washing basket. It came to her, looking at him, big men needed big rooms. Marsh, like his father before him, was six-three. At nearing thirty, very lean and athletic, whereas Sir Charles who had never appeared to carry an extra pound had somehow filled out with age. Both of them big men. Marsh's everyday gear was a bush shirt and jeans, a pearl-grey Akubra tilted at a rakish angle, his Cuban-heeled riding boots making him tower over the men. Today he wore a beautiful dark grey suit with a blue shirt and a silk tie, predominantly red, a matching kerchief in his breast pocket. In the city, as at home, he had the perfect male frame for hanging clothes on. Not that Marsh had ever shown the slightest vanity about his astounding good looks. His looks were almost irrelevant to performance. He had to shine academically, on the sports field, in the company of the rich and powerful. The focus had been on carrying on the Faulkner proud tradition. His mother and father, for all the differences between them, had been as one in their pride. Everything Marsh attempted he excelled at. Roslyn could not imagine what life would have been like for him had he not. Through the grace of God and bloodlines he was a born leader with a natural presence and an enviable capacity for getting the best out of everyone without friction.

Except *me*. Well, I'm not about to fall down and adore him, Roslyn thought. Those days are over.

"Quite the little achiever, aren't you?" Marsh broke into her thoughts.

"Why not? You showed me that, if nothing else. Sit down, Marsh, instead of towering over me. You make the place look like a doll's house."

"Sweet Rosa, it is, but it's pretty and comfortable and it's all you need. For now."

"And what is that supposed to mean?" She busied herself with the preparations for making coffee, thankful she had the best coffee beans at hand.

"Even you, Rosa, will get married. You vinegary little thing."

"I'll think about it when *you* walk up the aisle," she retorted dryly. "What's happened to Kim Petersen?"

"She's around." Idly he stroked the petals of a pink gerbera.

"No pride!" Roslyn clicked her tongue. "You've led her a merry dance."

"The hell I have! I made no promises to Kim."

Roslyn shrugged. "If that makes you feel better."

"I can't help it, Rosa, if women have only one thing on their minds. Not everyone is a dedicated career woman like you."

"My own woman," Roslyn told him with satisfaction. "Your sisters would have been all the better for a job."

"I agree." The tautness of his smile conveyed she had scored a point. "Being heiresses didn't help. I know you wanted them to feel guilty. Anyway they're married now and out of range of your tart tongue and superior IQ. You're a basket case feminist."

Roslyn paused with a hand on the coffee grinder. "You bet I am! All thinking women should have that in common. Your sisters are a throwback to the nineteenth century. So intelligent, yet with closed minds."

"Young women with large trust funds aren't always interested in making the most of their talents."

"Such a shame!" Roslyn sighed. "Anyway, they made sure I didn't dream above my station. I'm not likely to forget how Dianne behaved at her engagement party."

"I don't suppose the fact her fiancé was paying you too much attention had anything to do with it." Marsh stood up. "As always, your judgments are too trenchant. Here, I'll do that. You get the cups and saucers."

"I barely noticed him." Roslyn turned away to the cupboard. "I was only there at all to help Mumma." And glimpse *you*. Marsh, who had filled her eyes and heart.

"Well, I might accept that, but poor old Di couldn't," Marsh said. "The trouble with you, Rosa, you don't know anything about sexual jealousy. It's my bet you've sworn off sex altogether."

"I'm not prepared to talk to you about that!" she said tartly.

"So you're not going to tell me about the schoolteacher?"

Roslyn swung round with a look of surprise. "How do you know Dave is a colleague?"

"Come on, Rosa, wouldn't I check him out?" His tone was like silk.

"Sure you would. No problem, except you've never laid eyes on him."

Marsh ground the coffee before he answered, sniffing appreciatively at the rich aroma. "Darling, I spotted him on my last visit to school. A caring guy with a baby face.

He was coming out the main doorway as you were charging in like a baby rhino. Obviously you were showing your temper because he looked most solicitous. I can't think he knows what a little firebrand you really are. Crisp little skirts and button-up blouses aren't you at all. He should see you on Macumba riding like the wind. You might say you hate it, but it brings out your true colours.''

"Would you like anything with your coffee?" Roslyn asked in an abrupt change of subject.

"A little pleasant conversation." His blue eyes so riveting with his tanned skin and black hair never left hers. "Liv is most unhappy you've decided against coming. She's been looking forward to it immensely."

"Then why don't you give her time off so she can come to me?" Roslyn placed the coffeepot on the hotplate.

His dynamic face tightened. "You know perfectly well we have a full house at Christmas with a lot of entertaining."

"Ah, yes, the busy social scene!" she purred.

"Business and pleasure. There are people to be thanked. I couldn't do without Liv and she doesn't want to leave me in the lurch. No one will dare to give you a hard time."

"You bet they won't!" Roslyn replied with some aggression. "I'm a big girl now. Able to stick up for myself. Sock it back to them if I have to, but I don't want to live like that. No, Marsh, the further I keep away from you all, the better. I'll miss Mother terribly, but that seems to be my lot. Macumba comes first. It's been drilled into her. Sir Charles first. Now you. I should be used to it."

"Hang on a minute, Rosa," he said flatly.

"No, it's *true!*"

"What can I say to change your mind?"

"Absolutely nothing!" she maintained. "I'd like a little peace over Christmas. Christmas *is* peace, after all. Not a renewal of hostilities. The girls will be coming home, won't they?"

"For part of the time, yes. Would you like me to tell them to stay away?"

Roslyn shook her head, exasperated by his tone. "Never! They love you. They want you all to themselves. Part of the reason I don't plan on darkening your door."

"Because the past is with you at all times."

Roslyn poured the coffee and pushed it towards him. "Surely you're not suggesting we make a fresh start?"

"I'll even throw in the kiss of peace."

She could not focus on his face, the glittering, sapphire eyes. "No, thanks, Marsh. I remember your kisses. They're lethal. So far as I'm concerned, the past is always with us. Maybe not always on the surface but ready to spring to life at the slightest jolt. Our relationship is beyond repair. We came at life from opposite ends of the spectrum. You with a silver spoon in your mouth, the adored object of everyone's hopes and dreams. Me, the offspring of very ordinary folk. I know I'm easily given to anger where you're concerned, but I can't change that any more than you could have changed your mother's attitude. It impinged on us all. It colours Macumba to this day. There never was and never will be any question of my fitting in. It doesn't have everything to do with the fact you were the elite and we were so far down the social scale as to be off it. Your mother detested us. My mother and me. The way she used to look at us was just terrible. Anyone would have thought we were a threat to her. I was always waiting for the day she would accuse me of stealing—''

"Her son?" Marsh suggested abrasively.

"I don't think anyone would have stood for that. I was going to say the family silver. There was no rational explanation for it."

Marsh took a quick gulp of his steaming hot coffee and set it down. "Maybe for my mother there was. You could be too one-eyed on the subject, Rosa. Have you thought of that? My mother's life wasn't absolutely perfect. As a young woman like you, she would have started off her married life with high hopes, but somehow it all turned to ashes. When that kind of thing happens, it can have devastating results. I know my mother had a harsh tongue. She was very high-handed. But have you ever considered she might have felt herself a failure?"

In her total confusion Roslyn laughed. "A failure! Why, your mother considered herself quite extraordinary and in her way, she was. You Faulkners were the rightful rulers of this world."

"Leave it be, Ros," Marsh said, a decided edge to his voice. "If you want me to give it all up and go join a monastery practising poverty, I'm not doing it. You'd only find something else to chew on. You like to hate me. It makes you burn. And speaking of burning, would you mind putting the coffeepot down. Your hand is shaking so badly you're going to pour it all over the table."

"I'll do no such thing!" Regardless of her brisk denial Roslyn filled her own cup and returned the coffeepot to the stove.

"And while we're on the subject," Marsh continued, "you're too hard on Di and Justine. They're more vulnerable than you think. You said yourself Mother didn't take a whole lot of notice of them and Dad was far from demonstrative. *You* were the one he noticed. The girls didn't like it, either, when you grew more beautiful by the day. There's heartache in a face full of freckles and being too tall. Having a brother who supposedly got the lot. Mother was never gentle and loving with them. They felt her tongue just as you did, but unlike you, they never challenged her. I know you're not going to believe this, but Di in particular was terrified of bringing a guy back in case he caught sight of you. As it turned out, her worst fears were realised when Chris made an ass of himself at the engagement party. Face it, sweet Rosa, like it or not, you have a witching side to your nature."

She looked at him gravely, even sadly. "I was totally innocent of any charge of trying to 'bewitch' Chris, as your mother put it. I'm just glad she didn't have a stake handy she reacted so terribly. I've never set out to deliberately hurt anyone outside *you*. I'm pleased Di and Justine are happily married. They deserve some joy. I expect you to love and defend them. I'm even glad they'll be back on Macumba for Christmas, but I'm not running the risk of trying to hang out with them. They don't want me. The barriers remain."

"They will for as long as you let them. Do you know how bitter you sound, Rosa?"

That hurt her and she nodded wearily. "Unfortunately, yes, but unlike you, Marsh, I was wounded daily in my self-esteem. You'll never know what I'm talking about. It hasn't and will never happen to you. My scars don't heal. If I could get Mother to come to me, maybe they would. I love her so much but she seems to have some form of agoraphobia. She won't leave Macumba. It seems like the only place she's safe. Yet most of it has been terrible. I'll never, never, understand it. Ever since Dad was killed all I've ever wanted is to look after her.''

His expression was brushed with compassion. ''I understand that, Rosa, but you could hardly afford to keep her.''

''I'd give it my best shot. We don't live like you. We live quietly within our means. Besides, if she wanted to, she could take another job. Something interesting, part-time.''

''Like what?'' Marsh asked bluntly. ''Your mother is excellent at running a large house but she's had no experience in the workforce. Unemployment is running high and she's not the right age. You must realise she wants to be independent. Life is a lot different for her these days, Rosa. You should check that out.''

Roslyn took a deep, calming breath. ''No, thanks, Marsh. Charming as you undoubtedly know how to be, my mother is still your servant.''

''We don't use words like that anymore, Rosa,'' he said crisply. ''Haven't you learned?''

''My mother might appreciate that. *I* don't.'' She shrugged. ''I've carved out a life for myself, Marsh. A good life. I've bought a house and I have a secure, rewarding career. At this point I'm reasonably happy when happy is a mighty big word. It would be foolish and dangerous to allow myself to be drawn back to Macumba.''

''Yet you loved it,'' Marsh said, his expression faraway. ''There were times you were extravagantly happy. No one saw the magic of Macumba more than you. You knew all its secrets. You were addicted to the life, Rosa. That can't have changed.''

There was so much emotion in just being in the same room as him, Roslyn felt stifled. ''I've confronted that realisation, Marsh, but I've had to remove myself from the scene of so much pain and humiliation. Most of all, I've removed myself from *you*. You wounded me more than anyone.''

"You were a child, Rosa." His voice reflected a bitter regret.

"Old enough to give you pleasure."

Her arrogant Marsh visibly winced. "You wanted me as much as I wanted you."

"Yet you drove me away!"

"I *had* to!" Air hissed through his teeth. "It was a dangerous situation. The timing was all wrong. You were sixteen and I wasn't truly adult, either. Violent delights have violent ends, so they say, Rosa. How could I take you—"

"You *did* take me!" she cried, her voice rising passionately.

"I haven't forgotten. I was a savage then and wild for you. No one knew better how to tempt me."

"Of course!" She threw up her hands in disgust. "Woman, the eternal temptress. Woman destroying a good man's willpower. I *know* what I did, Marsh. How I acted. I abandoned myself to a fiery relationship. But I paid for it. God, how I paid for it. Afterwards you made sure I was kept out of the way. Macumba shut its doors. You started wooing a whole string of suitable girls. You even went to infinite pains to make sure I knew. Well, it didn't take me long to overthrow the old idolatry. Everything I felt for you sickened and died. You used me and I let you. I acknowledge that. But all that is left is remorse."

"Then it must be pretty powerful," Marsh challenged her bluntly. "You'd rather hate me than love anyone else."

The truth. The whole truth. And nothing but the truth.

It cut straight to Roslyn's heart. She sprang up, in her agitation knocking her coffee so that some of the hot liquid splashed across her hand. Instantly the fine skin turned red.

"For God's sake!" Marsh moved like lightning, overcoming her resistance and drawing her to the kitchen sink. He ran the cold water and held her hand under it. "Why do you fight me all the time? Fight yourself?" There was an angry, haunted look on his face.

"Maybe conflict is my natural milieu." His skin on hers was sending little tingles up her arm.

"Quiet, Rosa. Quiet." With infinite gentleness he dabbed a paper towel to her hand, miraculously as ever, concerned for the delicacy of her skin.

Put your hat on, poppet, and keep it on! How often had she heard him say that and adoringly obeyed? She felt such a longing for him; for the best days of her life, she almost cried out. The old magical link was running between them. Indestructible. She could see it in his eyes; echoes of a passion that had caused nothing but upset and pain. His nearness was intoxicating, trapping her. She wanted to touch him . . . hold him . . . take him to her breast.

"Rosa?"

He had broken her heart once. He would do it again. *Come to me, Rosa, my little love*!

The way he had talked to her! The world of ecstasy and wonderful dreams! What she had felt for him was a flame that had never gone out.

"Look at me," Marsh urged. "The pain will go away if you let it."

It might have been the devil himself at his most seductive and charming. A younger Marsh had been a

tempestuous lover. Now he was beguiling her with such
tender depth in his voice.

A fierce quaking gripped her. She could not move or
speak. She knew it for what it was. An erotic spell. Under
compulsion she raised her mouth and, as if at a signal,
a look of triumph blazed into his eyes.

"My beautiful Rosa!"

He was drawing her closer and closer, filling her with
a consuming passion. She made no outcry. Lean, caressing fingers bent her head back over his arm. Gentle,
but *insistent*. No guilt at all at having her at his mercy.
He was looking at her with such a mixture of feelings.

Conquest? Oh, yes!

Possession? Why not? Wasn't she Rosa, his little
captive love? It was her special role to please him.

This was the stuff of her dreams. The night-time
visions that fanned the terrible storms in her. She didn't
realise it, but her knees had buckled so badly he was
forced to take her weight.

A single lock had fallen away from his ink-black hair,
lying in a crisp curl on the polished bronze of his
forehead. His eyes were achingly blue, like the sky over
the desert.

"Rosa. Oh, Rosa," he whispered, looking—could it
be possible?—*vulnerable*.

It was all that she needed. She had waited a long time
for this. Pride and resolve streamed into her. She went
as rigid as a statue, revenge burning fiercer than love.
Once she had been a wild thing in his arms. Young, un-
tamed, clamouring for the rapture he had shown her one
perilous, desert night. Now she was breaking his power.
Exorcising him and the terrible fascination that had be-
devilled her for so long.

"Let me love you," he begged, frustrated by her withdrawal. His free hand had found the curve of her breast, cupping it. An ancient ritual that dredged up an involuntary moan. Eddies of dark pleasure began cascading in, lapping at her willpower.

"What is it?" he asked urgently. "Trust me, Rosa."

Trust him when he had dealt her such a terrible blow? Was he *mad*? Was *she*? The tenderness was no more than a manifestation of his mastery. An angry little sob escaped her and instantly he buried her open mouth beneath his.

Fever and delirium. All it had ever been. Trying to resist Marsh was like getting caught in a rip-tide. She would never have her freedom. Loving him, hating him, gave meaning to her life. For the moment she surrendered while ecstasy was repossessed.

"Rosa!" His low, agonised whisper came against her throat. "Don't tremble like that. I don't mean to—"

At that she jerked her head back. "You *do* mean to!" Her voice cracked with emotion. "As soon as you touch me, you mean to. You think I'm still a Faulkner possession. You can have me any time you choose."

"That's not true!" He denied it vehemently. "If it were, why haven't I laid a finger on you in years?"

"Because I've taken good care you don't!" She stared up at him, her arousal equal to his own. "Good grief, Marsh, don't you know how I hate you?"

"*Hate* me?" He almost spat it out. "Hate me, love me, what's the difference? Hell, I even like your kind of hate. You're a lost soul, Rosa, but you won't let anyone save you."

"Not *you*! I was your unquestioning victim once. Never again. I won't do *anything* to have you. Contrary to your expectations."

"Don't say any more, Rosa." There was a warning sparkle in his eyes.

"But there *is* more," she continued, quite unable to stop. "I'm fearful of coming to Macumba. I've said it's because of your extended family, who, with few exceptions, treated me and my mother like a sub-species. They took the view, of course, that they didn't have to bother their heads over the servants. But really, it's all to do with *you*. I don't give a damn about them and their place in the sun. You knew I was in love with you, long before I knew what being in love was. You were a god to me. Surely you saw that? The sun danced in the heavens every time you smiled at me. You had such powers. I placed all my trust in you. My life. If you looked into your soul, you would know that you had the power to destroy me."

A tremendous tension was all around them. His blue eyes glittered like gems. "You, Rosa?" he returned scornfully. "You call yourself a victim? You're strong and you're clever. You've fought your way out of a background you apparently detested. You were always too proud. Too ready to see insult where it wasn't really intended. So people are careless, insensitive? They don't always intend to wound. You've been as toey as a boxer since you were a child. If you imagine I've treated you badly, how do you think you've treated me? I'm sick to death of your bitter tongue. The way you want to lash me whenever I come near. I let you go. I had to. Both of us were thrown into a terrible, painful situation. The timing couldn't have been worse. So I was weak, with no thought in my head but having all the beauty and innocence you offered. I've suffered for it. Don't think I haven't. There's heartache and regret in every corner of my mind. If *you* loved me, *I* worshipped at your altar. There was no limit to my passion. But it was wrong and audacious. It had to stop.''

"So you could feel virtuous again? In control?'' Roslyn stared into his eyes, saturated in their blueness. "Besides, the scandal might have travelled far and wide. The heir to Macumba, Sir Charles and Lady Faulkner's adored only son having it off with the housekeeper's daughter. My God, who of the elite could grapple with that? Grounded in conservatism and doing the done thing.''

Marsh's striking face tightened. "As far as I remember, correct me if I'm wrong, the housekeeper's precious daughter did everything in her considerable power to delight me. Venus herself couldn't have been more alluring. You held me in your palm, yet you insist on playing the tragic victim. You always were a great one for histrionics. These past couple of years you've never let me near you. But you won't let go, either. What is it, the goddess syndrome? Believe me, I'm at the end of my tether. What is it you want, Rosa? Spell it out. *Marriage*?''

For a moment Roslyn looked as though the sky had fallen in on her. "Never in my wildest dreams did I expect that,'' she said finally.

"What did you expect?'' he demanded. "A lifetime of being my mistress?''

She visibly paled. Her nerves were worn ragged. "For a while... nothing... more. I was crazy with love for you. So young, so ardent, I couldn't hold back. We had unforgettable times. Secrets between us, but it's long gone. You hurt me too much and I can never forgive you. Right or wrong, that's the way it is. I can't even bear to be in the same room as you.''

"What about the same bed?'' he asked on a hard rasp.

She shook her head. "We never shared the same bed."

"Only the two of us locked under the desert stars. So what does it all mean? Liv has to suffer, too?"

Roslyn turned away, looking her strain. "We've been over and over this, Marsh. Even for my mother I can't walk back into the lion's cage."

He looked over at her, his blue gaze detached, even distant. "Not even as my wife?"

CHAPTER TWO

SHOCK immobilised her. Her heart rocked wildly, then seemed to shudder to a stop.

"I know," he said flatly. "It didn't sound romantic." In fact he was looking at her like a long-time opponent who had thrown down a challenge. "Maybe these last years have beaten the romance out of me. At any rate, I'm serious."

Roslyn, for all her intelligence, was looking as though she was having extreme difficulty tracking the conversation. "You're serious?" Her voice came out oddly pitched and full of confusion.

Marsh's brief laugh conveyed anything but humour. "Why the hell are you looking so stunned? For my sins, I am."

"Sins? Atonement? You must be mad!"

He nodded in perfect agreement. "For better or worse, you're the woman I want."

"Passion, Marsh. Nothing more." Her tone was pained and very subdued.

"I wouldn't knock the passion if I were you," he said sardonically. "In my experience it's pretty rare. I've never had a woman raise such hell in me. You've brains, courage, toughness. I admire your style. I even admire your wild nature though you do your level best to keep it under wraps. Under that satin skin lurks a primitive."

"Takes one to know one," she retorted instantly, but still in that subdued tone. Her eyes scanned his face, marvelling at the precise arrangement of features that made it so compelling. "This is madness, Marsh. You made your decision. So did I. They can't be unmade. Why, if your parents were still alive, you'd never propose such a thing."

He hated that. How he hated that, for his eyes flashed blue lightning. "I could have sworn you knew me. Now I realise you don't. I've never proposed to a woman in my life, but if I had, no one would have prevented the marriage. No one runs *me*!"

"So *you* say!" She reacted fierily. "Times might have changed, but your family didn't change with them. They believed in the old feudal system."

"Listen to me, Ros!" He took hold of her forcibly, fairly shimmering with rage. "Macumba has changed already. I'm the boss now. Chairman of the board."

She pulled away blindly. "I'm going into the living room, Marsh. It's too claustrophobic in here."

She rushed away while he followed her more slowly, taking the armchair opposite her. "I didn't realise you'd be so shocked." He studied her pale face.

"Not even a little bit?" Her topaz gaze was quietly ironic. "All we've been these past years is sparring partners."

He shrugged. "Be that as it may, I can't exorcise what we had together. Neither can you."

"Maybe we should see a psychiatrist to help us out?" Her lips twitched.

His expression lightened, as well. "I don't have the time to work on that. Neither, apparently, do I have the self-control to stay away. I need a wife and, in due course, an heir. It might seem like a big challenge for us to marry, but we're not afraid of challenges, are we? I can give you back the life you loved. The splendid thing we shared and understood. You used to call us twin souls, remember? Maybe if we try hard enough we can have that back. I promise you a free rein. Your own money."

"Don't try to buy me, Marsh," she said with quiet dignity. "I'm not interested in your money."

"To hell with my money, then! In your case, it counts against me. But it could make life easier and fuller for Liv."

"So now we come to it. *Blackmail!*"

His mouth compressed. "Not a terribly attractive view. All's fair in love and war. Liv is your mother. Aren't you the same girl who used to rail because she didn't have lots of nice clothes and places to go? We could take care of all that. You might get all up in arms about money, but having it does make people a whole lot more confident. Liv is a beautiful woman. She should give life and maybe the right man a chance."

Her thoughts exactly, but Roslyn wasn't about to agree with him. "Aren't you the one who told me you desperately needed her services for the holidays?"

Marsh gave her a sardonic look. "Maybe I exaggerated a little. I could always get staff. No one like Liv, of course, but competent enough. I'm really after *you.*"

"Goodness knows why!" She sighed deeply.

"A blind obsession." His voice was spiked with self-derision. "You're just hiding out as a schoolteacher. I've seen your face all painted with ochres, parrot feathers on your head. Who nagged Leelya for the recipe for a love potion? I know I refused to drink it, but you could have slipped it to me at another time. You were a tricky little thing."

At his words, nostalgia swept sweetly across her mind. Leelya, an aboriginal woman who wandered the station, had been the great friend and mentor of her childhood. Leelya had been a vast source of information about humans, animals, the birds of the air and the fish in the streams. Leelya had taught her all about the timeless land, the red desert, how to play the clapsticks and dance in mime. Because of Leelya, she knew scores of myths and legends from the Dreamtime, how to gather food, find water, so vital to desert life. Leelya had taught her how to make that love potion and she remembered the recipe to this day. She had been quite a herbalist, mixing it perfectly, but Marsh had made her deeply unhappy by refusing point-blank to drink it. She'd been around fifteen at the time. They were down by the sacred lake with its flotilla of pink waterlilies and black swans. She had never forgotten his amusement. The way he had teased her, not knowing a young girl could fall in love.

After that failure, she and Leelya had put their heads together to create a special spell. Powerful woman magic that really worked. They had shared their secrets silently, the old gin and the precocious, self-dramatising white child. It was Leelya who had painted her face and body with bright ochres. Leelya who had arranged brilliantly coloured bird feathers in a crown around her head. Again her plan misfired because Marsh had burst out laughing, asking where was the corroboree?

"Rosa?" Marsh's voice catapulted her back to the present. "Where have you gone off to?"

She gave her head a little shake. "I was just thinking about Leelya. How is she?"

Marsh shrugged. "I haven't seen her for ages. She's gone walkabout."

"She was a great friend to me."

"Co-conspirator, more like it! You and she were always cooking up spells."

"Some of them worked. Perhaps not in the way we intended."

"That's the danger with magic, Rosa. Leelya should have warned you. I'm flying back to Macumba on Monday. I'd like you to come with me."

"You were always driven, weren't you, Marsh?" she asked reflectively.

"Let's say, I don't like to lose. I'm asking you to be my wife. You're not going to find anyone else in this life."

He said it lightly, but she found it significant. "Isn't that a bit melodramatic?" She, too, played it coolly.

"You're not getting any younger, poppet. Twenty-five in January. For all your beauty, you could just get left on the shelf. You want children. I know you do. You're very good with kids. It's all very well waiting for Prince Charming, but you must have a few fears he mightn't even exist. Besides, you are so damned hard to please. I don't think any man could measure up to your exacting standards. Better the devil you know than the devil you don't know. I'm approaching the deadline myself. I can't find a single woman to delight me for more than a week at the outside. You're the one with that unholy knack. I know these past years have been rough, but I'm prepared to take you traumas and all."

"The question is, am I prepared to take you?" Roslyn returned. "I'd cut myself off from you."

"So why are the scars too much to live with?"

Roslyn blanched and immediately he closed the distance between them, sitting beside her on the couch. "The things we say and the things we mean! We humans are terrified of exposing our hearts." He drew her into his arms. "You still care about me, Rosa, just as I care about you."

"No!" She shook her head in denial.

"I have trouble with that."

She buried her head against his jacket. "It's all about what you want, Marsh. Always *you*."

"I want the glory days back, Rosa. I admit it. This standoff could go on forever. I have to make the decision for both of us. But I'm not going down on bended knee and I'm not taking any more hell for the past, either. We have to bury it to survive. If you like, we can draw up a marriage contract. You can keep referring back to it. I'll give you time, but if you decide yes, you'd better know I'll never let you go. No running off. No divorce. You and me for all time. No one else. No lovers. Treat that very seriously. I could bring myself to shoot anyone you got involved with. I'm serious, sweet Rosa. Mess with me and you've made a huge mistake. On the other hand, if you honour our agreement I'll do everything in my power to make you happy. I remember holding you in my arms and promising you the moon and stars."

"Wild words, Marsh." She turned up her face, her voice husky.

"I remember." His expression was intimate, intense, a little brutal. "So do you. Marriage might put us out of our misery."

"It could leave us worse off than we've ever been."

"*I* don't intend to walk out," he announced, almost grimly. "Think about that. Get it right. I won't let you go, Rosa. Our marriage will be forever. Rooted in the soil of Macumba."

Her eyes were liquid amber, her thick black lashes spiked with tears she couldn't control. She let her whirring head rest back against his shoulder. "And in true, dynastic style you'll want a son?"

"I want a family," he said. "I want sons and I want a daughter just like you so I can spoil her."

"This is *real*, isn't it, Marsh? I'm not dreaming?"

He tugged her hair very gently. "It's real."

"It's the last thing I expected to happen," she said. "I have to think about it very seriously. You've taken me totally by surprise. You broke my heart once. There's no possible excuse for me if I allow it to happen again."

"Try to be more positive, Rosa," he jeered softly. "We can't let the past warp our lives. The future is full of hope. Besides, you're my favourite girl. What more can I say?"

"Maybe you love me dearly?" she responded with a return to irony.

The dazzling blue eyes became hooded. "Love is a danger, Ros. It makes fools of us. A man can lose control and you know me. I like being master of the game. Besides, I haven't heard any love words from you. Let's stick with what we know. We have a long, shared history. You're at the center of my life until I die. I never asked for it. It just happened like something preordained. Neither of us is going to beat this thing and we've both tried. For all that, we speak the same language. Come back to Macumba with me. Enjoy all the things you used to love. You'll have Liv's company and mine. Once, I was able to speak to your heart."

She stared up at him, searching for words. "Marsh, you scare me," was all she eventually managed.

He lowered his head and pressed a hard, fierce kiss on her mouth. "That's the way it should be. A woman should be a little scared of her man."

His philosophy in essence. She'd been warned.

Long after Marsh had gone, Roslyn lay on her bed feeling totally strung out. Marsh's proposal had literally taken her breath. She couldn't believe it, given they had done everything possible to avoid one another these past two years. Marsh had spoken ironically of a "blind obsession." No piece of theatre, but a well-documented human condition. She could vouch for its existence. Passion...obsession...bound them together as much now as at any time in the past. Its grip was unrelenting. Only, if the truth were faced, she loved him. But the truth threatened her. Once confided, it put her instantly back into the position of suppliant. Marsh simply wanted her, like he acquired desirable properties and made no bones about it. Not that they weren't compatible in other ways but she was convinced he would never have proposed had his mother been alive. The violence of Lady Faulkner's opposition would have caused tremendous upset. Marsh's sisters would have felt compelled to follow their mother's lead. Likewise the extended family with a few exceptions. The housekeeper's daughter, child of a stockman who had been killed on the station, was hardly the sort of person to invite into a family whose position in society went back to the earliest days of settlement.

Except Lady Faulkner wasn't around. No one would have to bear her violent opposition. Roslyn groaned aloud. She was so confounded by the turn of events she couldn't seem to think properly. She imagined her reaction was pretty much the same as someone who inherited a fortune right out of the blue. She had spent years trying to get over Marsh. Years of building up a defensive shield. It had been an absolute waste of time. She had only to see him, to hear his voice, for all the old longing to start up again. Her heart defeated her every time. Even her acquired persona of coolness and competence was unravelling at breathtaking speed.

"I'm in shock, damn it!" she told the empty room.

How could she seriously be considering a marriage between them? A monstrous thought in the old days, what had suddenly changed? Marsh had thrown off the constraints of family? Didn't she still *burn* with resentment? Their past was complex and painful; their future promised stormy times. She would always be the butt of someone's snide little joke, human nature being what it was. There was something else, as well. She was forced to consider it with some trepidation. Marsh was one of the richest men in the country. Not only did he control Faulkner Holdings, he had inherited the bulk of his mother's fortune, which stood at some 50 million dollars at her death.

There was a whole side to Marsh's life she knew absolutely nothing about. A side she didn't want to know about. Great wealth wasn't a great blessing in her view. No one could have called the Faulkners a happy family though even Lady Faulkner had played down the exact size of the family fortune. Strictly speaking, the beef cattle chain was down the list of interests. There was a massive investment portfolio. Marsh was one of the biggest shareholders in the giant Mossvale Pastoral Company. It was common knowledge. She didn't give a hoot about any of it, but Marsh was deeply involved in all Faulkner operations. Business trips took up a great deal of his time. In his own way, he was a celebrity even if he took great care to keep a low media profile. The Faulkners she knew were private people, hiding their wealth, not splashing out on a lavish lifestyle. Nevertheless, Faulkner money had built hospitals, schools, townships. They funded numerous charities, scholarships, and a major art prize. As heir to the trust, Marsh had worked for and acquired degrees in economics and law. In many ways he had been brought up like a prince in a castle, but immense pressure had always been placed on him from the earliest age. It was a heavy burden he had been forced to carry, but necessary for someone who would one day wield a lot of power.

That day had arrived. In keeping with tradition he was expected to take the right wife and raise a family. The right wife surely meant someone of similar background; in other words, one of the ruling classes. Not a schoolteacher of no social distinction at all. Worse, a skeleton in the family closet. Roslyn murmured aloud her distress. Once, as a child, she had overheard Lady Faulkner and Elaine Petersen discussing quite seriously and calmly a possible marriage between their children. Marsh would have been sixteen at the time. Kim, a year or so younger. It would bring two prominent families together. Cement already-rock-solid fortunes. Even then, Roslyn had been appalled. Did these women think they owned their children? Marsh didn't even like Kim Petersen. He had told her so.

That was *then*. Marsh and Kim had been an item only a few years back, when his parents had been alive. Lady Faulkner had long since given Kim her stamp of approval and she was a lifelong friend of his sisters'. One hundred per cent suitable. Absolutely top drawer. Kim wouldn't sit idly by while she trapped their adored Marsh. She would be branded the ultimate opportunist. Was she equal to the battle that surely lay ahead? If only he had said he *loved* her. If only...

Saturday morning she went shopping for presents for her mother. Saturday afternoon she spent in the garden in the warm sun planting out masses of white petunias along a border. At least she no longer felt stunned. Marsh had asked her to marry him. He had asked no one else. Hadn't she always prided herself on her fighting qualities? She would make him love her. She would bear his children. She could do absolutely anything so long as he backed her. She could return pride and happiness to her mother. Warmth and hospitality to a Macumba that had felt Lady Faulkner's brand of rigid exclusivity for too long. Nothing worth having was achieved easily. It all took hard work and commitment.

She glanced with pride around her garden. It was very pretty, if of necessity, small. The gardens at Macumba were magnificent, watered by bores sunk into the Great Artesian Basin. Lady Faulkner had had no time for the garden, preferring to leave all decision-making to Harry Wallace, a roving Englishman who had come to Macumba to play polo and stayed on as the resident landscaper.

She supposed in a way she hadn't been a *containable* child, because she had seen herself as absolutely free to roam the station at all times. Lady Faulkner had positively discouraged her. Sir Charles and Marsh had been extraordinarily indulgent, almost applauding her audacity. If only Lady Faulkner had been a kindly woman! Life would have been very different for all of them.

CHAPTER THREE

IT WASN'T until they were flying into the Faulkner desert stronghold that Roslyn fully realised what she was letting herself in for. She had come to Macumba all those years ago as a humble stockman's daughter, now she was seriously contemplating becoming its mistress. A rags-to-riches story. Something one might read in romantic fiction. It seldom happened in real life.

Seen from the air, the blood-red terrain was extra-ordinary. It stretched away to the rainbow-hued mesas on the horizon, the hills a vast network of caves that were the repositories of aboriginal art many tens of thousands of years old. Macumba was fabulous. Even in drought savagely beautiful but so empty and isolated after her quiet leafy suburb it might have been a strange, new planet. Down beneath them were knife-edged rising temples of shimmering red sand, crystal-clear rock pools, swamps and billabongs that were a major breeding ground for nomadic water birds. Where the coolibahs stretched their long limbs over the water, colonies of ibis, spoonbills, shags and herons built their nests and the brolgas performed their wonderful dance on the sands. In the good seasons countless thousands of ducks invaded the swamps, becoming a common sight.

The outback *was* birds. The phenomenon of the west, the budgerigars in their chattering millions, the brilliant parrots, the soft galahs, the zebra finches, crimson chats, variegated wrens and huge flocks of white corellas that often appeared to decorate trees like giant white flowers.

So often she had sat and watched the soaring flight of the great wedge-tailed eagle over the dunes. This was the place she loved most in the world and always thought of as the real Australia. The land of whirlwinds and mirage, its ancient plains crisscrossed with a vast natural irrigation system that allowed the country's huge cattle kingdoms to support their stock. Roslyn thrilled to it in every fibre. But as they flew in, Marsh at the controls, she braced herself for conflict. What they were considering was a radical shift from tradition. She could bring no fortune with her. No powerful family alliance. She could only bring herself. She was of the mind and generation to think it ought to be enough. She had no inflated ego, but she knew she was good-looking, intelligent, healthy. Most people found her pleasant. She was highly regarded as a teacher. She hadn't anything to be defensive about. Times had changed. She was entitled to a better life than her mother, yet she knew the instant Kim Petersen found out she was back on Macumba, Kim would fly in ready to do battle in her cool, superior way. Kim was the natural successor to Lady Faulkner. Kim was one of the self-styled Higher Order.

"We're home!"

Marsh's announcement brought her out of her reverie. His voice was filled with great satisfaction. *You're* home, she thought.

"No premature announcements, Marsh," she begged. "I want to gauge reaction to my return in my own way. Once the family arrives, it's bound to be forthcoming."

"You're not marrying the family, you're marrying *me*."

"It's never as easy as that." She sighed. "You and your relatives are very close. You're bound in so many ways. Blood, business, shared heritage. You're the anointed heir. They all love you. They don't love *me*. I don't expect them to, but I do want to be seen as a person in my own right. Not the little kid who tagged after you.''

''Give it a rest, poppet,'' he said.

''I want nothing more. At the same time I'm compelled to defend my own position.''

''You're good at that, Rosa,'' he drawled. ''You always were as sharp as a tack. While we're laying things on the line, might I suggest you lighten up. You're too ready to fly off the handle. The girls would have made friends with you long ago were you not so touchy. They admire you, in fact. Your beauty and your brains, the way you've made a career for yourself. Marriage has improved both of them, you'll find. They've matured and mellowed. *Mellow*, you ain't!''

''A subjective view, Marsh. I don't have trouble with other people. It will do you no good to criticise me.''

He made a grab for her hand and kissed it. ''Forgive me, my lady. Tolerance is the wisest course for both of us. Anyway, there's Aggie.'' He referred casually to his distinguished grand-aunt Dame Agatha Faulkner, author and historian. ''You and she usually get on like a house on fire.''

Roslyn smiled with uncomplicated pleasure. ''Dame Agatha is a true lady. She brings out the best in everyone. Everything was so much nicer when she visited. She was even interested in what I was doing. She's a great feminist. Always championing the rights of women. She was the one who discovered I was musical, remember? She always asked me up to the house to play for her.''

''Darling, take it I'll carry on the tradition,'' Marsh said suavely. ''I can just picture us. You with your lovely head bent to the keys. Me, relaxing in my favourite armchair, a single malt whisky in my right hand. Peace. Harmony. I like anything you play."

"I thought you said it was torture listening to me practice," Roslyn accused him.

He glanced sideways, blue eyes sparkling. "I lied. Secretly I was envious of your talent." Lined up with the all weather runway, he released the landing gear. "This is a great day for us, Rosa. Be happy."

The late Lady Faulkner had been a splendid horse-woman and a champion show jumper in her youth and had continued Macumba's tradition of breeding and training high-quality polo ponies for the home and international market. It had proved a lucrative sideline to Macumba's beef trade. The breeding and training program continued under Joe Moore, head of Macumba's veterinarian laboratory. It was a venture Roslyn the horse lover had always been interested in, but Lady Faulkner had made sure she was barred from the stables complex except for the times Sir Charles himself had intervened on her behalf. It was Sir Charles who had once said she could sweet-talk any horse on the station, a gift she had inherited from her own hapless father.

Her father's grave was in the station cemetery. She had looked down on it as they flew in. Her thoughts spiralled back to the day they had buried him. It had been the worst of times, two days before Christmas. Her beautiful mother had been white to the lips, so overcome by grief she had to be led away. An image of herself arose, huddled against Marsh, a devastated young girl just home on holidays. She had tried desperately not to break down. Her father had always called her his "little cobber" and she told herself she had to be brave for him. It was Marsh who had drawn her quite unselfconsciously into his arms, telling her to let the tears come out. She might have been his little sister so closely did they remain, she sobbing and sobbing, he stroking her long curly mop of hair tied with a black ribbon. Marsh had been there at every turn. Woven into the fabric of her life. Marsh had listened endlessly to her dreams *and* her rages. They shared the same sense of humour. They had been the greatest of friends.

Adolescence and the swift onset of sexuality had changed all that. One day she was an innocent child. The next, a budding woman barely able to cope with the intensity of her changed feelings. The Marsh she had looked on with great pride and pleasure, her dearest friend, her hero, was now the person she was terrified of being close to because of the tumultuous feelings that engulfed her. Marsh had often given her a fleeting kiss on the cheek, coming and going, or when she had been especially helpful around the place; now she wanted to turn up her mouth to him. To feel the delicious edges of his sculpted lips. She wanted his hands on her flowering body. He was totally, perfectly, acceptable to her. He could do what he liked.

Such a situation had only one consequence. He *had*. It was only when he turned away from her, she wanted vengeance. Even contemplating marriage she still wanted it at some subterranean level. It was a dilemma of the heart she would have to address. On the trip up to the homestead Roslyn looked around her with hungry eyes. There was no disrepair, no neglect on Macumba. The bungalows, sheds, the men's kitchen and canteen, the schoolhouse, the huge stables complex with its white-railed rings and horse paddocks were maintained in prime condition.

Silver-boled ghost gums grew in abundance as they approached the main compound, the homestead set like a pearl in many acres of formal and informal gardens. A small stream, a tributary of Macumba Creek, which in flood became a river, girdled the house, widening out to a lake in front and several ornamental pools as it wandered on its way. It was an enterprise begun by Marsh's great-grandmother, Charlotte, Surrey born and widely travelled. The indomitable Charlotte, horrified by the vastness and "utter savagery" of her new environment had taken to conquering it with a passion. She had worked tirelessly to create a wild garden. Any thoughts of a decent garden in a semi-desert environment was plainly out of the question. Yet she had succeeded so well her name had become legend. Over the years the gardens had become more formalised with built-up terraces, archways, fountains, beautiful statuary and an Indian summerhouse by the lake.

The effect was quite extraordinary coming as it did on the desert approaches. But nothing could surpass the sheer romance of the homestead for Roslyn. She had loved it as a child. She loved it still. Her blood always quickened when she saw it. It rose out of the grassed terraces like a great white bird with its wings outstretched. There was the central colonnaded core, two long projecting wings. The stone pillars were perpetually wreathed in a white trumpet flower that blossomed prodigiously. It was only looking directly towards the portico that Roslyn was assailed by one of her visions.

The shade of Lady Faulkner. She stood just outside the front door with its lovely fan lights and side lights, tall and imperious in her riding clothes, swishing that well-remembered riding crop.

Don't come in here, my girl, she warned. You are not and never will be good enough for my son.

Roslyn's slender body tensed as it had done so many times in the past. What a powerful woman Lady Faulkner had been. Despising frailty in others but driven by her own devils.

"What *is* it?" Marsh demanded, catching sight of her expression.

"I thought I saw your mother. She was standing right outside the door."

"You and your imagination, Rosa," Marsh said in a neutral voice. "There's no one and nothing to hurt you."

"I never did feel comfortable walking into the homestead."

"I thought you loved it?"

She shook her head. "I didn't say I didn't love it. It mightn't love me."

"Nonsense!" Marsh drew the Jeep to a halt. "Nothing is beyond you, Rosa. You're a million times stronger than you know." He turned to her, his blue eyes glazing with vitality. He looked profoundly pleased to be home. He swooped on her luggage and pulled it out onto the driveway and as he did so a middle-aged man in khaki trousers and a matching bush shirt came through the front door and hurried down the short flight of stone steps.

"Don't you bother with those, Mr. Marsh. I'll take 'em."

Roslyn swung around, extending her hand. "Ernie! How good to see you."

"Good to see *you*, Roslyn." Ernie Walker, part aboriginal, and a fixture around the homestead, gave Roslyn his white, infectious grin. "The place ain't the same without you."

"I've brought you something." She met the liquid, dancing eyes.

"Don't tell me. The latest Slim Dusty?" Ernie named his favourite country and western singer.

"Don't tell me you've got it?"

Ernie shook his head. "Woulda had it, though. Thanks a lot, Roslyn."

Roslyn held up her hand. "A present for all the kindnesses you poured out on me."

"Saved your hide plenty of times and that's a fact!" Ernie agreed. "You were one hair-raisin' kid."

They all looked back as Olivia Earnshaw, "Mrs. E." to just about everyone on the station, rushed through the front door, arms outstretched.

Roslyn immediately took off like a gazelle, so the two women fell into one another's arms at the top of the stairs. Roslyn rained kisses on her mother's cheeks, while the ready tears collected in Olivia's eyes.

"Darling, let me look at you!" Olivia peered beyond Roslyn to Marsh. "I just knew you'd bring her back."

"He's not a man to take no for an answer. You look wonderful, Mumma," Roslyn said. "You never age a minute."

And it was almost true. Seen in the streaming sunlight, Olivia Earnshaw looked a decade younger than her fifty years and still beautiful. Her skin was unlined except for a few fine wrinkles around her sherry-coloured eyes. Her thick black hair worn carelessly short was as glossy as her daughter's and only lightly dusted with silver. Her body was as slim and erect as a girl's. Looking at mother and daughter, one was struck by the extraordinary resemblance, but whereas Roslyn's face hinted at banked-up passions, Olivia's conveyed a certain natural docility.

Marsh looked from one to the other, his thick black lashes veiling his expression. Roslyn could be as obdurate as a Shetland pony but there was nothing she wouldn't do for her mother. Liv was as enchanted with her daughter as ever. Both women were equally protective of the other. Both had suffered under his mother's hands. Though he had loved his mother and understood the demons that drove her, he had to accept she had done a lot of damage. It was for Roslyn to decide if she would allow the scars to heal.

They had a marvellous evening together with Marsh playing host. Harry Wallace, resplendent in a cream safari suit with a silk cravat rakishly tied at the throat, came up from his bungalow to join them, delighted to see Roslyn and savouring Olivia's company for all she chose to misinterpret it. They had drinks and a platter of delicious canapes in the cool of the veranda and an hour or so later, dinner, which Olivia set up in the family room, a lovely spacious room half the size of the formal dining room, made all the more beautiful since Marsh had had the rear wall demolished and replaced with floor-to-ceiling French doors and Palladian fanlights.

Tonight all the doors were open to the wide expanse of terrace and the breeze drifted in, totally seductive with the wonderful aromatic scents of exotic and native flowers.

"That was a marvellous meal, Liv!" Harry proclaimed, admiration in his hazel eyes. "Cooking is an art form."

"So's landscaping. You're a genius, Harry."

"Am I ever!" Harry accepted Olivia's accolade as his due. He was a very *interesting*-looking man in his late fifties, not handsome, but whipcord lean, his good

English skin tanned to leather by the elements, rapidly thinning fair hair but a luxuriant moustache; a man women would always find attractive. His speaking voice was one of his greatest assets, cultured, resonant, full of a dry, tolerant humour. From his earliest days on Macumba he had been treated more as a family friend than an employee, even by Lady Faulkner. Roslyn always thought it had a lot to do with his voice, so upper crust, and his easy, self-assured manner. Later on she suspected it was her mother as much as polo that kept Harry on the station.

"You know, Liv," he now confided, "it's always been an ambition of mine to open a restaurant in some fabulously beautiful place. North Queensland possibly. Glorious country. A clifftop overlooking the blue sea and the off-shore islands. I could build it and create a beautiful garden. You could supervise the cooking. Of course, you'd have to marry me."

"The things you say, Harry!" Olivia brushed the suggestion off as a joke.

"I think he's serious, Liv," Marsh said dryly.

Olivia only responded with a gurgle of laughter. "He tells me something different each time he sees me."

"Marriage is always the bottom line, m'dear," Harry said gently. "Sooner or later you'll take that in."

Roslyn glanced quickly at Marsh, vivid as a flame, and he winked, obviously used to these exchanges. Roslyn looked back at her mother. Olivia's head was bent, her creamy cheeks flushed with the wine and sheer pleasure. She looked especially lovely tonight, Roslyn thought proudly. She could take her place anywhere. She was wearing the dress Roslyn had bought her, a simple wrap dress with little cap sleeves and a longer skirt, but the printed silk was beautiful; multicoloured sprigs of pansylike flowers on a white ground. It had been very expensive and it looked it. Mumma deserves the best, Roslyn thought fiercely. She had bombarded her mother with presents, but her main present was still tucked away for Christmas. Olivia wore her new Lancome makeup, too. Giggling like a couple of schoolgirls, Roslyn had made her mother sit still while she'd applied it. It brought Olivia's lovely gentle features to full life. Even her expression had the dreamy tenderness of a film star.

What a waste! Roslyn thought for perhaps the umpteenth million time. My mother is a beautiful woman. She should have a full life. Perhaps it could still happen. If Roslyn married Marsh, her mother would be assured of comfort and security. She could travel, do anything she liked.

They talked until nearing midnight when Marsh and Roslyn decided to take a stroll down to the lake. A huge, copper moon hung low in the sky and the white summerhouse took on a magical, romantic aspect.

"You know Harry's serious," Marsh said as they walked. "He's been in love with Liv for years."

"Mumma doesn't think of him in that way," Roslyn answered, not without regret. "We can't love to order."

"She's very fond of him just the same. She could be even fonder but she won't let him close."

"Surely Macumba's housekeeper, if not respectably married, has to live like a nun?"

"You don't quit, do you?" Marsh said, with no bitterness in his voice but a question.

"I'm sorry." Roslyn took a deep breath, feeling remorse. "We've had such a lovely night. Mumma is so happy."

"But unfortunately for Harry her thoughts don't encompass remarriage."

"Love is grief, Marsh," she said. "Maybe Mumma, like me, yearned for the stars."

"What does that mean?" He glanced down at the dark head near his shoulder.

"Are you sure you don't know?"

She waited for his reaction and it wasn't long in coming. "Let it lie." They had been walking arm in arm and she felt his muscles bunch.

"That's no answer, Marsh. Just something else to be swept under the carpet. Sir Charles was the fixed star in Mumma's firmament."

"As *I* recall, Liv was devastated by your father's death."

"I'm talking about *after* my father died. Mumma was so bereft and lonely. She wasn't exactly surrounded by a supportive family. She was virtually an orphan with an orphan's mentality. And there was your father. A man among men. You could hardly blame her. She made a decision and in a split second lives changed. Your father became too important to us. We orbited around his star. But he couldn't give Mumma anything. He was a married man with a family. A deeply conventional man. A pillar of society. He'd made his commitment and I accept that as right and proper. I pay full reverence to the sacrament of marriage. I'm only saying *our* lives were ruined. My mother somehow sidestepped life, while mine has been overflowing with conflict and resentment."

"God knows that's true," Marsh agreed with bleak humour. "We're none of us angels, Rosa. If Liv sometimes wept for the impossible, you might consider my father had his bad days, too. No one had to open my mother's eyes, either. She knew she had been found wanting quite early in her marriage."

Roslyn threw up her head, quite agitated by his words and their implication. "What are you saying, Marsh?"

He shrugged, backing off. "All families have secrets, Rosa. Unhappiness can make people cruel."

"But your mother was unkind to her own daughters!" Roslyn, a witness to countless incidents, stated.

"Maybe she saw them as an extension of herself."

"How, in what way?"

Marsh let a moment pass. "The knowledge that they were like her," he said. "You thought my mother didn't love my father. You got that wrong. He dominated her every waking moment. Theirs might have been as close to an arranged marriage as one can get, but my mother never could accept my father hadn't come to love her as she loved him. There was no visible alienation, but she needed to take her unhappiness out on someone. And there was Liv. Liv and her beautiful little daughter. Right under her nose and in a position of deference."

"It was cruel, Marsh."

"Lord, yes!"

"There *was* no relationship, either!" Her voice trembled traitorously. "My mother had a clear conscience. She has never done anything dishonourable in her life."

"I hope you're not suggesting my father might have made life difficult for her?" he said curtly. Worse, with some arrogance. *His* exalted father could do no wrong. *His* mother's sins could be easily pardoned.

Incensed, Roslyn broke away, walking rapidly towards the lake. "Heaven forbid!" she called.

Marsh caught up with her, turning her to face him. "Can't we take this calmly for once?"

"It seems not. And don't call yourself calm. You're as arrogant as the devil. The fact is, Mumma wasn't grand enough, anyway. She was a *servant*. There was always that as a powerful deterrent." She stopped abruptly on the hard constriction in her throat.

"It's impossible for you to let go, isn't it?"

Roslyn felt something akin to frenzy run through her blood. Why was *she* always in the wrong? "Listen, that's no news flash," she proclaimed angrily. "I don't say to the past, 'come back and haunt me.' It does. Your way seems to be to put a lid on it, but you can't keep it from simmering away. We have to address this, Marsh."

"When it might destroy us? It's already robbed us of years. My parents, God rest their troubled souls, are dead."

Sudden tears swam into Roslyn's eyes. She shook her head. "I'm sorry, Marsh. I want so much for things to be right between us, but my mind is full of trepidation. I'm on the classic emotional roller-coaster. Nothing is going to be easy for us. Particularly me. I'll be the target. We can't simply go off and get married. Just the two of us. Everyone will expect a big ceremony. The media will have a field day with my rags-to-riches story, my whole background. The gossip mongers will have plenty to say in private about your father and my mother. There will be plenty of ugly speculation. Honourable as they might have been, any halfway observant person could have detected they really cared for each other."

Marsh lifted his head and looked away across the lake. "There's little enough caring in the world, Rosa. I have to tell you I don't give a damn about what people think. The people that matter anyway will understand. You'll have to be the same. If you want us to be married privately, we will. I'll marry you any way you like."

She heard the resolution in his voice. "Then the word will go around I'm pregnant. I really can't win. By the same token, I don't feel inclined to duck anything, either."

"That's my girl!" He drew her to him and kissed her hair. "Besides, I think I'm entitled to see my wife as a bride. It would give me infinite pride and pleasure. I want everyone to see you, Rosa. The whole world!"

It was the reassurance she wanted. Harmony was restored. By common accord they walked into the summerhouse, its romantic ambience increased by the fragrance and starry profusion of the King Jasmine. It twined through the white latticework and climbed the slim, elegant supports.

"How beautiful it is here!" Roslyn leaned her hands against the railings, staring out over the shining expanse of water. The lake was alive with myriad little sounds and the incessant throbbing song of the cicadas.

"Beautiful!" Marsh came behind her, wrapping his arms around her.

Marsh, the sun in splendour. Marsh, the moon at night. At his slightest touch, the heat of desire blazed up. In the soft, purple darkness she could make out the outline of two swans, probably Sirius and his mate, Bella, asleep on the water, their necks bent over their backs. The other swans were somewhere on the banks, their black plumage hiding them from sight. The lake was deceptively deep. Once she had given in to a craze to dive in and Sirius, the most splendid and aggressive of the swans, had chased her.

"Do you remember when—"

"Sirius chased you? Yes, I do. I don't know how many times I told you he would." He pushed the shining cascade of her hair to one side, revealing a profile traced by the starlight in silver.

A soft, smouldering sensation was licking along her veins. "You promised, Marsh."

He kissed the exposed side of her neck, one hand roving the sweet curve of her breast. "I certainly didn't promise not to put my arms around you."

"That's all it takes."

"With *you*. No one else. You're a creature of fire and air. You know how to weave spells." His mouth began nuzzling her ear, the tip of his tongue tracing the delicate inner whorls.

"It's late," she said.

"Yes, I know."

Her hands half floated up to stop his, then dropped as yearning overcame her. She rested her head back, savouring afresh his marvellous, male scent. It had always aroused her. She had a boundless urge to turn into his arms, to feel the fused lengths of their bodies. He continued to kiss her as though famished, dozens of kisses, light, delicate, pressing. She let him, her mind reliving the old splendour in total recall. The very same stars looked down on them then as now. Brilliant, eternal, their radiance lightening the black velvet sky to a soft, mysterious dark lavender. No other sky looked like the sky over the vast, empty outback. The air was so pure, so unpolluted, there scarcely seemed a barrier to reach up and pluck a star. A perfect jewel.

She gave a dreamy, spellbound sigh. "Marsh, this has to stop."

"When did I ever force you to do anything you never wanted?" he murmured.

She could think of no time at all. The fire in the blood had been mutual. Her magnetism for him had been as electric as his magnetism for her. She knew she was brushing too close to danger. Only when he told her he loved her could she cast off the final constraints.

She was suffocating with emotion now, her feelings building to crisis point after the long deprivation. Water lapped against the giant grasses and reeds. A breeze shook out the jasmine, spilling blossom and scent.

"Kiss me," Marsh said, nudging her face up to him. "Kiss me and don't stop. It's been too long."

Her breath fluttered. Her lips parted. She turned her body slowly, a near balletic movement that had him reaching for her, his body hard. Masterfully he sought and found her mouth spreading a white-hot illumination that enveloped them both.

"Sleep with me, Rosa. Sleep with me. I'm afraid to let you go."

At his words, the sound of passion in his voice, she felt herself at the brink of a chasm. She had done what he wanted before and lost everything. She could risk it all now. She pressed her hands against his chest, immediately fending him off.

"I'm no sex object, Marsh."

From lovers to instant antagonists. A pair of aliens.

"Here we go again," he said harshly. "You're a lot more than that."

"Tell me, please. I have to know. What has changed exactly that you now want to marry me?"

"Why exactly are you considering my proposal?" he countered in a suave, cutting voice. "I thought we had this out?"

She felt tendrils of the jasmine clutch at her hair and she brushed it off. "I'm sorry, but we've never had anything out. Not since you drove me away. I certainly wasn't good enough for you then."

"Don't talk like a fool," he said angrily. "You were a schoolgirl."

"Well, there's *that*," she said, her voice deceptively benign. "I had an excellent education. That helps."

He heard the hard mockery behind the dulcet tone. "Indeed it does. Then there's the way you look. The way you speak. The radiant flash of your smile. There's not a man alive immune to the spell of a beautiful woman. Men are erotic creatures, Roslyn. Violently erotic at times. I can't promise to keep you up there in your ivory tower. I want you badly. You, on the other hand, won't be truly satisfied until you bring me to my knees."

"How repulsive!" Roslyn actually recoiled.

"And too damned close to the truth. You'll never admit to it, Rosa, but revenge drives you. I was hopelessly in love with you, but you saw yourself as a woman scorned. Damn it, girl, you were a teenager. *Sixteen*!"

"I was a woman in all else. I knew how to suffer. I'm damaged, Marsh," she said in a hurt, aching voice. "Can't you see that? Damaged people are dangerous, so they say."

"Hell, Rosa, you talk as though you've stumbled on a secret. Lots of us are damaged. I was fairly well damaged myself. There wasn't a lot of love in our house and what there was wasn't normal. In my parents' eyes I had to be perfect. The perfect heir. I wasn't a medal to be worn with great pride. I was just a boy like any other. Many the time I would have swapped places with my friends. To hell with my inheritance if it was going to cost me my only chance at happiness."

Roslyn shut her eyes to all the emotion in his voice. "I know the pressures that were put on you, Marsh."

"So stop hammering away at me. I want to marry you, Rosa," he said, revealing the ruthless, imperious streak that was in him. "Not only that, I'm going to. You're *mine!*"

CHAPTER FOUR

LATER that night, alone in her bedroom, Roslyn sat on the bed trying to think how best to tackle the difficulties that lay ahead of her. The very first thing she had to do was liberate the minds of Marsh's family who had never recognised her worth, but had chosen to see her through Lady Faulkner's jaundiced eyes. In the old days, she would scarcely have been allowed a place at the table. Now the fact that Marsh had asked her to marry him represented an overwhelming triumph. The only trouble was, there was lots of pain behind the triumph and lost time.

Engulfed in her thoughts Roslyn gave a start when her mother tapped on the bedroom door, then put her head around it.

"Sorry, darling. You gave a little jump. I just wanted to say goodnight and tell you how wonderful it is you're here."

"Come and talk to me, Mumma," Roslyn begged, patting a place on the bed beside her.

"Just for a little while," Olivia smiled. "You must be tired out after all that travelling?"

"I ought to be, but I'm not. Too many things on my mind." As Olivia found herself a comfortable place on the bed Roslyn slipped a pillow behind her mother's head. "You looked beautiful tonight, Mumma," she said proudly. "The dress suited you perfectly. Harry couldn't take his eyes off you."

"Harry enjoys women," Olivia said in a complacent voice, taking her daughter's hand.

"Of course he does, bless him, but don't hide your head in the sand, Mumma. He's very fond of you."

"Harry knows he's perfectly safe with me," Olivia said, as she always did, but added another piece of information. "He was married. Did you know?"

Roslyn was astonished. "He's never said a word."

"Well, it's a sad story." Olivia gave a sigh. "His wife left him for his best friend. She was awarded custody of their two sons. They were six and eight at the time. Harry hung in for some years but somehow his ex-wife managed to turn the boys against him. He had access, of course, but mostly when he wanted to see them she had the boys doing something else. She blocked his calls, made his visits a nightmare. The younger boy started having tantrums. When the children started calling his former friend "Daddy" he decided he would have to try for a life of his own. He was 'someone in the city', whatever that might be. He didn't elaborate and I didn't ask. He left the boys well provided for, then he took off. There doesn't seem to be a place on earth he hasn't visited. Even Antarctica. He spent a lot of time in Kenya then he travelled on to Australia. He's attracted to the wide, open spaces."

"So poor old Harry is one of the walking wounded," Roslyn said with sympathy. "He must have been heartbroken."

"He was. Still is. The bonds weren't broken entirely. The children became men. They wanted to repair the relationship. Harry sees them when he goes back to England. One's in law, the other works for a merchant bank. Neither is anxious to get married."

"It does happen to the children of broken homes."

Olivia gave her daughter a tender look. "You've got something on your mind, haven't you?"

"Am I that transparent?" Roslyn smiled.

"I'm your mother, darling. I know all the signs."

"My beautiful mother!" Roslyn lifted her mother's hand and kissed it. "I don't know how you're going to take this, but Marsh has asked me to marry him."

"Roslyn!" Olivia's nostrils flared and a look of acute unease spread over her gentle face.

"I thought that might be your reaction." Roslyn let out a deep sigh. "It's been a long, long attachment."

Olivia frowned. "As if I didn't know! It was quite terrifying the way you two were so crazy about each other. I expected at any moment Lady Faulkner would cast us out into the desert."

Roslyn smiled wanly. "She just didn't have enough clout. Sir Charles would have said no. He wasn't a man to argue with."

"Nevertheless he was worried. You, particularly, were so *young*. It had to stop."

"Yes, indeed!" Roslyn said in a cynical voice. "We all know about these old families. So very closely knit and so conservative. They don't favour the nouveau riche joining the family let alone the daughter of people who work for them."

"No matter how beautiful and well-educated," Olivia added sadly. "You have to consider, Rosa, Marsh's family is important to him. He's tied to them in every possible way. Macumba is only a small part of the Faulkner interests now. They knew the benefits of diversity before a lot of their friends started to think about it. There's a huge property portfolio. There's Mossvale. The family has a major holding in Westfield Mines.

There's a whole lot more, I'm sure. They're very private people."

"I'm not marrying Marsh for the money. It doesn't concern me."

"Then it should!" Olivia looked at her daughter almost sternly. "You could be thrust into a whole lot of responsibilities, even a lifestyle you mightn't want to handle. You won't be living quietly here at Macumba. Increasingly it will become a more public life. It would be easier, too, if Marsh or even his father were self-made men. New Money. But they're the Old Rich."

"Mumma, I hate these labels."

Olivia shook her glossy head. "Unfortunately they exist. We know that better than anyone. The Old Rich have a well-developed herd instinct. They like to stick together. They don't favour outsiders. As soon as an announcement is made, the press will be onto it in a flash."

"So none of us led a life of crime. What do we have to hide, Mumma? We're perfectly respectable."

"Maybe we won't be by the time they tell the whole story. You know it won't be easy, Rosa. You *know*."

"So you're saying, don't marry him?" Roslyn asked wryly.

"I'm saying my main concern is your happiness. You've had a hard enough time of it."

"I thought you loved Marsh?"

"I do!" Olivia compressed her soft lips. "He has never in all these long years offered me the slightest hurt. He shielded us both from his mother's tongue. The girls, of course, followed their mother's lead . . ."

"I think they were afraid *not* to."

"Possibly. But can't you see, darling, Marsh has always lived like a feudal prince. What Marsh wants, he gets. He even has his own private kingdom. He's uncompromising when it comes to his possessions. I know how the two of you suffered when your affair was broken up. I know how you worked to put it all behind you. I know the determination and the pain. Marsh seemed to want a clean break, as well. He courted Kim Petersen for a time. She was Lady Faulkner's choice for her son's bride. Yet here you are! The two of you can't seem to leave one another alone."

"That's passion, Mumma."

"Then passion is a damnable thing!"

"It doesn't make for an easy life. I've tried to form other relationships, Mumma. They didn't work out. Marsh was always there standing in the shadows. No one could come near him let alone surpass him."

Olivia's white brow furrowed. "But can he make you happy?"

"If we put aside his family, Mumma, we're two of a kind."

Olivia continued to brood. "Not just his family, Rosa. A wide circle of friends. Your news is dazzling, darling, but I can't say I'm happy about it. Some will try very hard to break it up."

"Would they dare with Marsh?"

"They'll go behind his back. You know how it works. You've been the target of so much unkindness," Olivia reflected with some foreboding.

"So have you! Why didn't we go, Mumma, while we had the chance?"

"You're strong, Rosa. You're a fighter. I never was. So I did nothing."

"And afterwards you came to care for Sir Charles?"

"Ah, don't!" Olivia made an agitated little movement.

"We can be honest with each other, Mumma."

"I loved your father, Roslyn."

"I know you did. I'm talking about later, Mumma. I understand. Our lives were caught up with the Faulkners. You were young, beautiful. There was too much proximity. The Faulkners didn't have a happy marriage. Everyone thinks Sir Charles was a great man. I say he should have set you free!"

There was sadness and old despair in Olivia's eyes. "The decision was *mine*, Rosa. I wanted to remain. I told myself I needed the job. And I did. But in a way it was self-deception. Sir Charles offered me a job out of the goodness of his heart. It was a genuine act of kindness. I mourned your father. I still do, I will never lose his memory. I will never lose the memory of Charles. There was nothing dishonorable between us. You must believe that."

"I do, Mumma."

"We cared for each other, but we were separated by a great chasm."

"Sir Charles was *married*, Mumma. Marsh isn't."

"No, but he's practically supporting the whole damn lot of them. I'm telling you, Rosa, if the family can figure a way to stop this marriage, they will!"

"Then they're in for a few shocks," Roslyn said determinedly. "I know there'll be stormy days ahead, but Marsh has asked me to marry him and I've told him yes."

"Then if that's your decision you have my total support." Olivia's beautiful eyes suddenly filled with tears. "You're a hundred times brighter and stronger than I am."

This lack of self-confidence in her mother affected Roslyn deeply. "I wish I'd met that stepmother of yours. I'd have given her a piece of my mind."

Knowing her daughter Olivia could see precisely how. "She would never have crushed you the way she crushed me. You have your father in you. Lots of grit."

"It's an easy matter for an adult to crush a child, Mumma," Roslyn pointed out gently.

"I suppose!" Olivia's mind turned inwards. "She used to play games. She was sweet to me in front of my father and so unkind and critical in his absence. My father thought I was the one who wasn't trying. That's what separated us in the end. He took her part against me. People do play games, darling. Especially women. You'll have to be on your guard."

"Why do you think I was sitting upright in bed? I was trying to figure out the best way to go."

"Well, you won't have much time. The family arrives next week. As Christmas comes closer we can expect lots of visitors. The Petersens among others. When are you going to make an announcement? I don't even know if you're engaged."

"I told Marsh I wanted a little time. I want to gauge their reaction to my being back."

"Are you sure that's wise? Why not present them with a fait accompli?"

"No." Roslyn shook her head. "I want them to *reveal* themselves first."

"Count on them to do that," said Olivia. "And count on an uproar when you make your announcement."

"Well, I am expecting a few adverse comments," Roslyn drawled.

"So what's going to happen to *me*? I don't imagine Marsh will want his mother-in-law around the place?"

"Why ever not?" Roslyn looked startled.

Olivia had to laugh. "Not the three of us, darling. I just can't see it. A young couple, newly married. You'll want to be on your own."

"But I want you here, Mumma," Roslyn said in dismay. "This is a *huge* house! If we wanted to, we needn't meet up for months."

"Oh, darling," Olivia shook her head. "I'm finished as a housekeeper. Am I right?"

"Absolutely!" Roslyn sprang up from a lying position to kiss her mother's cheek. "You've worked for the Faulkners long enough. I want you to be able to enjoy yourself. I want you to be financially secure."

"Ho, ho!" Olivia said warily.

"No 'ho, ho,' about it! Marsh wants to settle my own money on me. I'm entitled to it as his wife. What's mine is yours. You've always wanted to take an overseas trip with Ruth. Now you can do it. You can do anything you like."

"Oh, lord!" Olivia moaned. "I'm a quiet person. This is going to change everything."

"Yes it is, Mumma. We'll have to convert overnight to grand ladies." She laughed aloud, an infectious sound that made her mother laugh, as well. "Personally I don't believe we have to do much converting. Maybe a new wardrobe."

"Promise me I wasn't part of it, Rosa?" Olivia asked in a low voice.

"What do you *mean* Mumma? Looking after you wasn't part of a package deal. It's a side benefit. I've always loved Marsh. I always will. Consider it something neither of us can do anything about."

"It can happen like that. So when exactly do I cease my duties?"

"I wonder if you can get breakfast?" Roslyn joked. "No, seriously, Mumma, as of now. I can cook almost as well as you can. We'll share things until we get a capable woman or perhaps a couple. The house girls are used to me. There'll be no problems."

"Except you won't be 'little Rosie' anymore. You'll be Mrs. Faulkner. All the station staff will have to adjust to that. Harry will take it in his stride. He's always said you could take your place anywhere. For myself I'd just as soon stay 'Mrs. E.' when the family arrives. Going social could give me severe palpitations."

"You can do it, Mumma."

Olivia thought for a moment. "Darling, it's quite possible I could find it a nightmare. It's too big a change. I'm the housekeeper. Not an old friend. Am I allowed to talk to Marsh about this?"

"Of course!" Roslyn exclaimed. "We want your blessing, Mumma."

"If only my blessing would make a difference!" Olivia sighed. "I'm not the matriarch of the family."

"You don't have to be so modest, either." Roslyn clicked her tongue. "You're a lady, Mumma. A *real* lady. You're the dearest, most important woman in the world."

"My baby!" Olivia pulled Roslyn to her and held her. "I've succeeded with you, if nothing else. So when *is* it you're going to make your announcement? Knowing Marsh, I'm amazed he's giving you any time at all."

"He plans to tell them Christmas Eve."

For a long moment they remained wrapped in each other's arms.

"Then look out for the shock waves," Olivia said finally.

* * *

The week before the family arrived was undoubtedly a happy one. For the first time Roslyn had the complete freedom of the station, which she and Marsh toured from dawn to dusk as business partners, a new thing in Roslyn's life. Marsh had already begun a crash course of instruction. She was given an overview of the station's current management plan and the horse breeding program. As well, he had taken to filling her in on the seemingly endless list of family business interests, which for the most part she had been unaware of it. It had all been part of a far-removed dreamworld the Faulkners lived in. It had nothing to do with her.

Now she discovered with Marsh as her mentor she was able to assimilate a whole mine of information and ask the sorts of penetrating questions that clearly pleased him. She had a good mind and Marsh made it all sound so *interesting* she was able to absorb a surprising amount of fact and figures as well as a few cautionary tales. The money Marsh talked was mind-boggling. How could anyone possibly spend it? Marsh didn't see it that way. He was the custodian for future generations. There was a serious philanthropic program in place, part of which she already knew, but it would be a long time before she felt she would have a good working grasp of the Faulkner money making machine.

One thing had emerged. Marsh had an unswerving dedication to what he saw as his destiny. Was destiny for males alone? Roslyn was thrilled and reassured Marsh had decided to take her into his confidence, but she wanted to use her own voice. She had sailed through her arts degree and diploma of education. It wouldn't hurt her to undertake further external study in the coming year. Business management or commerce. The Faulkner business holdings were ten times bigger than she had im-

agined. If she really wanted to involve herself in Marsh's
life, and it seemed that was what he wanted, she had
better prepare herself for a share of the power. Someday
their child would take on the custodian role. The
Faulkners had held strictly to the old feudal rule of
primogeniture.

Roslyn was of the generation to believe women were
capable of big things. Why shouldn't a *daughter* assume
the role of custodian when the time came? A daughter
could do it. For herself Roslyn didn't want to sit back
and become one of the Faulkner pampered women. That
would be the worst thing. Excluded from the 'men's talk'.
She knew for a fact Marsh's sisters had not been encouraged to take an active interest in the family's business
affairs. Not only that, they hadn't been reared to think
of themselves as achievers. Roslyn didn't want that to
happen to her and it certainly wasn't going to happen
to any daughter she might have. Further study was in
order. If she wanted to be listened to, she had better
know what she was talking about. The prospect didn't
scare her. With Marsh so much on her side she saw lifting
her game as a challenge. It was the others who would
do their best to shoot her down. Well, good luck to them!
She had lived a lifetime subjected to unkind and unfair
criticism. It might have made her prickly but it had also
made her strong.

Marsh and Roslyn were out on one of their exhilarating
dawn rides when Marsh brought up the subject of his
sisters' pending arrival. They were riding parallel to the
silvery green waters of Mali Creek with the breeze skit-
tering around like a happy child, fluttering the leaves
and the swamp grasses, scattering blossom—a pure white
bauhinia clung like a symbol to the fine cotton covering

Roslyn's left breast—and ruffling the glassy surface of the water breaking up reflections of the flowering trees. Both of them had slackened the reins of their horses, allowing the spirited animals to walk, and now Marsh seemed anxious to talk.

"It could be, Rosa, you're making things more difficult for yourself," he remarked, adjusting the rakish angle of his Akubra as the sun gleamed across his sapphire eyes.

"You're like Mumma." Roslyn shrugged. "You want to present them with a fait accompli."

"I don't need my sisters' permission to marry."

"You'd like their approval, though."

"Of course, but I'm not going to crack up if they're not absolutely thrilled."

"Let's face it! They won't be *pleased*."

"I had a sinking feeling when Di decided to marry Chris. As far as that goes, Justine's husband nearly puts me to sleep, but I've had to accept them."

"But they are very *very* establishment."

"Times change, Rosa."

"For anyone in the real world."

"You're saying my sisters are locked away?"

"It's a closed world of privilege, Marsh. You know that."

His handsome mouth went wry. "I guess when you get right down to it they don't know how the other half live. It's the luck of the draw, Rosa. To compensate we do our bit as a family."

Roslyn nodded. "The rich have a moral obligation to help out as best they can."

"Then do allow us to take some credit," Marsh said in a dry voice.

"For heaven's sake, I *do*!" Roslyn looked up as a flight of parrots as brilliant as flowers streaked from the sweet-saped trees. "I don't expect you to sell off everything."

"I'm not going to. Even to oblige you," Marsh said lazily, reaching down to pluck a wild plum which contained more vitamin C than any other fruit. "Isn't it a glorious morning?" Beneath the wide brim of his Akubra his eyes glittered like gems. "Here, have a bite."

Roslyn took the plum and tasted of its tangy, dark gold flesh. "Have you thought the girls are bound to ask Kim Petersen over?"

"I can't see that will do any great harm. They've been friends forever." He leaned sideways in the saddle, caught her face and turned it to him. "You've got juice on your chin."

"Lick it off."

"I intend to." His tongue collected the pearls of moisture then moved over her parted mouth. "When are you going to sleep with me?"

She let him kiss her, a convulsive little shiver moving through her body.

"When we're *married*."

He drew away and laughed. "What if I run right out of control?"

"You won't!" She gave him a challenging smile.

He continued to stare back into her eyes and the smile stole away. "Promise?"

"Not a hope!"

She felt the lick of heat move through her body and enter her cheeks. "Kim will be devastated when she finds out about us."

"Then I'm sorry!" Marsh sat his horse splendid as a feudal king. "These things will happen. Anyway, I got through to Kim long ago. She ought to accept Craig McDonald before he turns to someone else. That's the best offer she's had all year. Lord knows, I never told her I loved her. Or that I wanted to marry her."

"Unfortunately for her she was reared to believe you *did*."

Marsh clicked his tongue in exasperation. "Blame it on our foolish mothers. What do you really think this holding off is going to achieve?"

Roslyn rapidly veered her horse away so it wouldn't trample a clump of purple, cream-throated lilies. "I *told* you. I want to gauge your sisters' reaction to having me back."

"I'm sure they can handle it if you don't press them too hard."

"What's that supposed to mean?" Roslyn's topaz eyes flashed.

"Now, now, Rosa, you'll have to wrap up that aggression."

"I don't like getting hassled," she said more mildly.

"Do you know anyone who actually *does*? Another thing that concerns me. When is Liv going to give up playing housekeeper?"

"She's shy about her new role. Do you *mind*?"

"Such a feisty little creature!" He glanced at her beautiful face. It was full of feeling; his own fierce joy in the morning. "Tell me, what's happened to the buttoned-in schoolmarm?"

"Scratch me and you'll find she's in."

"So, I'll volunteer."

It was said tauntingly and her body thrummed with response. Many times this past week his arms had gone around her, caressing, possessive, his murmured love talk sweet and hypnotic. Many times she had half expected he would override her soft, stifled protests, but in the end he had always released her, knowing full well she could hardly contain her desire. When he held her there was only his *touch*. His inescapable magic.

Masses of bauhinia blossom tumbled down on their heads. Marsh swept off his Akubra, dislodging the floral butterflies caught in the wide brim. "I'm not going to wait long, Rosa," he told her with a sort of thrilling finality. As always he had read her every expression. "We've wasted enough time. Two months from the engagement, we'll be married."

She felt a frisson of panic, then a great curl of rapture. "How am I going to organise a big wedding in *that* time?"

"I honestly don't know. You *want* a big wedding?"

"Yes, I do!" Her voice shook a little.

"You'll make an unforgettable bride!" His eyes swept over her, amazingly sensual, amazingly blue.

"It's a fantasy, isn't it?" Even now she was experiencing a sensation like dreaming.

"More, it's a marriage," Marsh answered almost tautly. "Two months should be long enough for a clever, well-organised girl like you."

She nodded, her mind racing pleasurably ahead. "It will take a lot of planning but if we know what we're looking at."

"Well, you won't be inhibited by a lack of money," he teased dryly. "I thought we'd be married here on Macumba if you feel the same. We'd have to throw some sort of super party in Sydney for those we can't fit in."

"Macumba will be fine." Who, then, would invite the shade of the late Lady Faulkner? Roslyn thought. "Where would we go for our..." She was aghast she couldn't get out the word.

"Honeymoon, Rosa?" His voice was almost tender. "Don't be shy. Anywhere in the world you want to go. Our marriage and honeymoon will be a very important part of our lives."

"Well, then, just the two of us on a tropical island," she said.

He turned his head swiftly. His eyes gave off such brilliance! "You're serious?"

She nodded. "I'm stunned this is happening at all."

"I'm walking around in a bit of a daze myself." His laugh was deep and amused. "If you want a tropical island for two, that could be arranged. On the other hand I'd like to ensure your comfort at all times. Perhaps as an alternative we could cruise the islands of the Great Barrier Reef. The Whitsundays. It's a dazzlingly beautiful world. We could visit your uninhabited islands, anchor in a turquoise lagoon, make love on a secluded beach, pull into one of the luxury islands for a romantic dinner. Actually, it sounds great, but so would a trek across the Great Stony Desert with you as a companion."

Intense joy flooded her. "So you'll be skipper?"

"Aye, aye, ma'am!" He saluted her lazily, yet the depth of expression in his eyes drenched her in blue. "You can leave it to me to organise the honeymoon. All you have to bring along is you and maybe a pretty dress for when we have dinner."

"I'll make certain I have one and a swimsuit besides."

"Throw in a sexy nightgown." He smiled. "Then I'll have the pleasure of taking it off."

"I never could trust you."

"You can trust me when we're married," he said, very intensely. "Make no mistake about that. But never, never, look at another man."

"And if I do?"

"You'll regret it," he said promptly.

"I didn't mean it, Marsh." Her response was hardly more than a whisper. "It's always been you."

"And I fell hopelessly under *your* spell. We're going to make this work, Rosa. Our marriage will be forever and ever." Deliberately he lightened the severity of his tone. "Now, I'm on my way home for breakfast. Juice, fruit, steak and eggs, maybe some hash browns thrown in. Plenty of toast and coffee. Are you coming?"

Roslyn's topaz eyes gleamed. "Not only that, I'll beat you back."

"You *think* so?"

Roslyn's hand clasped the reins, gathering them in. "I'm going to give it my best shot!"

The challenge was taken up, ending in a passionate kiss as the victorious Marsh lifted her from the saddle and led her from the stables complex up to the homestead.

CHAPTER FIVE

MARSH was the first to spot the charter flight carrying his sisters when it was only a speck in the cobalt sky.

"That's them now. Right on time!" He thrust up from his planter's chair, his handsome face filled with animation. "I might as well drive down to the strip. Sure you won't come, Rosa?"

Roslyn felt the familiar flutter of nerves in her stomach but her voice was perfectly serene. "No, thank you, Marsh. You go ahead. The girls will like that. We'll wait for you here." She stood to see him off, going to the wrought-iron railing that enclosed the veranda and leaning her slight weight against it.

"Right!" He leaned down and kissed her, the expression in his eyes bringing the heat to her cheeks. "You're not a bad-looking girl, are you?"

"Glad you've noticed."

"Do you remember a time I didn't?" His fingers moved lightly around her magnolia throat.

"Now now, you two!" Olivia called from her comfortable wicker chair.

Marsh gave her a mocking salute. "All right, I'm off. Ten minutes at the outside." He took the front steps of the homestead two at a time.

"Did you ever see such a graceful man!" Olivia sighed. The Jeep swept down the drive before she went to join her daughter at the railing. "Do I really need to stick around, darling? I'm getting bad vibrations already."

84

"We have to think positive, Mumma," Roslyn said, trying to sound bracing.

"Easy for you, difficult for me." Olivia gave a little wry laugh. "With the exception of Marsh and Dame Agatha, all the Faulkners give me heartburn."

"A teaspoon of apple cider vinegar in a glass of water. That's the cure."

"I've been known to take it occasionally." Olivia smiled. "Marsh is so pleased they've come. Say what you like, the family is very close."

"Tell me about it!" Roslyn invited dryly. "If you're too nervous, Mumma, you don't have to stay."

"Then I'd be leaving my little chick on her own." Olivia slipped an arm around her daughter's waist. "Marsh is right. You look lovely."

"That's good. I went to a bit of trouble."

"You have a natural chic, a natural style," Olivia said, regarding her.

Roslyn was dressed simply in a silk knit sleeveless top and fluid wide-legged pants, both in a subtle shade of gold that placed enormous focus on her eyes. Because of the heat, her dark hair was confined in a Grecian knot, the severity of the hairstyle only serving to draw attention to the purity of her bone structure.

"Of course, it's handy to have a beautiful mother," Olivia said playfully.

"You can say that again! The most beautiful mother in the world."

"Oh, it's lovely being together!" Olivia leaned her head against her daughter's. "You fill my aching heart."

"It does ache, Mumma?" Roslyn turned her head to stare into her mother's eyes.

"That sort of slipped out, darling. What did I want from life anyway?"

"A lot more than you got!" Roslyn's topaz eyes flashed.

"Sometimes when you start off badly, the pattern continues," Olivia said. "Even today I dream of my own mother. So many dreams! So many people in them. All dead."

"It's time to be happy now, Mumma," Roslyn said, gripping her mother's hand. "I want you to enjoy life."

"As long as I wasn't part of the bargain, Rosa. I happen to know you'd do anything for me."

Roslyn didn't answer for a moment. "It's no hardship marrying Marsh."

"It's not going to be easy, either. Why should *you* have to fight for approval?"

"A lot of people have to do it, Mumma. I have to be strong. Prove my worth."

"And they have to prove nothing."

"That's the way of it! The first hurdle is Di's and Justine's visit."

"Then count on a little unpleasantness, darling. I know you never saw it, but the girls were very jealous of you when you were all growing up. They weren't dealt much of a hand when it came to their looks and they had to compete with you for their *father's* as well as their adored brother's, attention. It doesn't make for easy relationships."

"I felt for them, Mumma. I still do. But they never wanted my friendship. Things will have eased now they're married."

"If only I had complete confidence in that!" Olivia sighed. "I'm dreading Chris's arrival. He did make such an ass of himself over you."

"I never *saw* him, that's why. Indifference was the big turn-on."

"Well, don't say I didn't warn you."

Beyond the main compound the Cessna was commencing its descent. Under ten minutes later the Jeep swept back up the drive with Marsh at the wheel, Dianne beside him and Justine in the back seat. Both young women were wearing wide-brimmed straw hats to protect their sensitive skin and both had a hand clamped to the crown.

"Come on, Mumma, enough of this idle chitchat. Let's get this show on the road." Roslyn stood to attention and, smiling wryly, Olivia did the same.

"What do you bet they've got enough luggage for six months?"

"Try ten cents. Ernie will have a big job getting it all into the house. There he is now." Roslyn looked to where their aboriginal houseman was rounding the west wing.

"Ernie's definitely got eyes in the back of his head," Olivia said.

Marsh parked the vehicle and his sisters stepped out. Dianne was the first to look towards the veranda and as she did so she appeared to give a start.

"It doesn't look as though Marsh told them you were here," Olivia remarked in an ironic voice.

"I wanted it to be a surprise."

"A surprise it is, my darling. You saw *that* with your own eyes. Justine was always the nicer girl. Go down now. I'll wait here like a good housekeeper, hands folded quietly in my nonexistent apron."

"You've been getting very cheeky lately, Mumma." With a smile fixed on her face, Roslyn walked down the stairs and out onto the circular driveway where Marsh and his sisters stood in a tightly knit group.

"Why, Roslyn, this is a surprise!" Justine, the perfect lady, held out her hand.

"How nice to see you, Justine." Roslyn took it, her smile including the younger sister who stood almost scowling. "Di, how are you? I hope you both had a pleasant trip?"

"Hi, Roslyn!" Dianne said in her clipped voice. "No, not really. I can't understand how anyone could call Jock Bannister a good pilot. I thought I was going to be sick at least three times." In fact she didn't look well. Her strong-featured face showed strain. She was wearing a smart, tobacco linen dress that should have suited her but somehow didn't. Her one beauty, her thick, curling tawny hair, was cropped to within an inch of its life.

"A cup of tea will soon put you right," Marsh said soothingly. "Go up out of the sun. I'll give Ernie a hand here."

"Anything *I* can take?" Roslyn couldn't keep her eyes from straying around the amazing amount of luggage.

"Ernie will take care of it," Dianne informed her none too politely.

Justine sought to make up for it. She took Roslyn's arm. "Spending the holidays with your mother, Roslyn?" she asked as the three young women walked towards the house. "Marsh didn't think to tell us you were here."

"Mostly it was a surprise."

"It was a bit!" Justine admitted with a faint smile. "I must say you look marvellous. You get more beautiful every time I see you."

"Yes, and isn't it a bore!" Dianne cracked out in her arrogant voice.

"Behave yourself, Di," her sister urged.

"No such thing ever happened to us, did it?" Dianne said almost angrily. "Marsh is the most gorgeous man you ever saw and we turned out two scraggly ugly ducks.''

"Which is why you had your hair chopped off," Justine retaliated. "Good hair, too. Don't you think, Ros?"

"Yes, I do!" Roslyn looked at her, her expression both serious and helpful. "That particular tawny shade is quite rare. Both of you have the height and the features to carry off a mane. Men always go for long hair anyway."

"Well, you'd know!" Dianne said with a short laugh. "It must be years since you've visited us. It's a wonder you could *live* without seeing Marsh."

"I don't think he found it easy not seeing me, either," Roslyn replied gently. She kept her expression unflustered while she fought down the little spurt of anger.

"So put that in your pipe and smoke it, Di!" Justine looked at Roslyn almost admiringly. "Don't take too much notice of Di's ill humour. She's been like that for weeks."

"What she means is, I'm preggers," Di announced.

"Why that's wonderful!" Roslyn turned to Dianne with pleasure.

"It might be if I could stop feeling sick."

"Oh, you will!"

"You'd know, would you?" Dianne answered rudely.

"It's generally accepted the first three months are the worst. When is the baby due?" Roslyn asked.

"If I can believe anything my obstetrician tells me, August."

"Chris must be thrilled?"

"He *is*," Dianne confirmed with triumph. "As far as I'm concerned, it's a bit early in the marriage for me. I wanted a little bit more time alone, but he must have his son and heir."

"Let's hope you're not carrying a girl," Justine said tartly. "It's got to be a *boy*, Ros, didn't you know?"

Dianne sighed. "All I'm hoping for is a healthy child."

They had reached the veranda where Olivia, a graceful figure in a white, sleeveless blouse and a button-through denim skirt, stood waiting. "Hello there, Mrs. Earnshaw!" Justine called as they mounted the steps to the veranda. "It must be wonderful for you to have Roslyn come to visit?"

"Lovely!" Olivia smiled. "How are you both? Well, I hope?"

"You'll hear about it so I might as well tell you. I'm pregnant," Dianne announced as though no one else had ever had that experience.

"I'm delighted for you, Dianne," Olivia responded in her gentle voice. "You must be a little tired after your journey. Would you like tea?"

"We'd *love* it, Mrs. E.!" Justine swept off her wide-brimmed hat embellished with masses of dried flowers. "What about here in ten minutes?" She indicated the spacious veranda with its charming arrangements of white wicker armchairs and glass-topped wicker tables.

"I want to go up to my room," Dianne said in almost her late mother's tone of voice. "Have Ernie get a move on with my bags."

As a consequence of Dianne's attitude Olivia did her best to cry off sitting down to dinner, but Marsh insisted.

"I won't have you off by yourself," he told her emphatically. They were in the kitchen where Olivia and Roslyn were making preparations for the evening meal. "I shouldn't have agreed to this charade in the first place."

Dianne's abrasiveness had thrown them all off balance. Marsh included. "Dianne is pregnant, Marsh." Olivia moved to the oven and popped in a chocolate pecan torte. "I don't want to upset her."

Marsh's handsome face tautened. "She's only been home a few hours and she's succeeded in upsetting everyone else."

Olivia looked more worried than ever. "Can't you see she doesn't want us around, Marsh?"

"Nothing changes," Roslyn said. "Well, that's not true. Justine is really making an effort to be pleasant."

"I'm rendered dumb by such jealousy," Marsh frowned. "Maybe it's genetic and not taught. I don't understand it. I honestly don't!" His eyes gave off an angry shimmer.

Roslyn went to him and put a hand on his arm. "Be gentle, Marsh. Justine told me there was a little pressure put on Dianne to have this baby before she was ready and maybe because of it she's been plagued by morning sickness."

"Then implore her to take her medication!" Marsh sounded exasperated. "Her doctor wouldn't have given it to her unless he was sure it was safe. Di always did like making things difficult for herself. I've asked Harry to join us, as well. Harry can keep the conversation going in the most difficult situations."

But even Harry's amazing conversational powers were put to the test. They were all assembled in the study, Marsh's now, which the family often used for intimate gatherings. It was a large, beautiful room, panelled in English oak with wonderful Pompeian-style frieze, lots of pictures, books and trophies, the armchairs and sofas upholstered in jewel-bright tapestry weaves to lift the dark lustre of the woodwork.

"Nothing for me, thank you, Marsh," Dianne said with exaggerated resolve. "I'm determined to do this thing right."

"Why do you make so much out of everything, Di?" Justine groaned. "Marsh was only going to offer you a Perrier water. You could easily manage it, surely?"

Dianne's long nose quivered. "Maybe a small glass." She glanced across at Roslyn sitting quietly in a wingback chair. The light from a nearby lamp fell in a gleaming crescent across her cloud of dark hair and creamy skin and Dianne felt the old jealousy bearing down on her in a giant wave. "Are you joining us this evening, Roslyn, or are you having dinner with your mother?"

Roslyn felt the familiar bitterness of rejection rise in her throat. It was downright scary how like Lady Faulkner Dianne had become.

"We're all having dinner together," Marsh said before Roslyn could formulate an answer. For a second he showed a formidable disapproval to his sister. "Liv and Harry often keep me company when I'm on my own. I don't see why they shouldn't now. Friends make things so much better, don't you think?"

Dianne didn't answer for a minute and Roslyn, for one, held her breath. "It's *your* house, Marsh." She sounded as if he'd betrayed her. "I was only *asking*."

"Perhaps you could play for us after dinner, Roslyn?" Justine intervened hastily. "I've always envied you your musical talent. Mother was so disappointed in us. Every time I touched the keys my hands got clammy. Di could barely squeeze out a tune, yet Grandma Marshall was a fine pianist. Two of her brothers played to concert standard. The Faulkners were musical. Aggie was supposed to have been a brilliant pianist in her youth. Her teachers wanted her to make a career of it but her father wouldn't hear of her going away to Europe to study. She had to become a writer instead.''

"Roslyn can certainly thank Aggie she can play now,'' Dianne said in a sharp, superior voice.

"And how is *that*?'' Roslyn was confused and startled. It was an odd sort of remark to pass, even for Dianne.

"Encouragement,'' Marsh supplied, giving his sister a glinting glance. "Agatha always encouraged you, Rosa. Every time she visited she had you up to the house to play for her.''

"Yes, she did.'' Roslyn's confusion began to recede, but it didn't disappear. "She was always very kind to me.''

"You make it sound as though you were surrounded by people who weren't?'' Dianne asked, glacier-eyed.

"That's how I *felt*, Dianne.''

"To my intense shame I recall that was so,'' Justine said with a regretful expression. "We needed to take that line to please Mother, God rest her soul. I've often thought about it and I realise I didn't really want to, but Mother could be fairly terrible if one didn't see things her way.''

"How dare you speak about Mother that way!'' Dianne snapped, shocked.

"Is this all news to you, Di?'' Justine asked in a goaded tone. "We know exactly the way Mother treated Roslyn.''

"It's all in the past, Ju-Ju.'' Marsh reverted to his childhood name for his sister. "We can't go back and change anything, but we can all start a new life. That's certainly what I intend to do. Harry, what about another martini?''

"I won't say no." Harry stood up in some relief and offered Marsh his cocktail glass. "You know exactly how to make 'em. Just show the vermouth to the gin."

It was nearly impossible to get Dianne to join the conversation at dinner. Halfway through the main course she suddenly thrust back her chair, holding herself very erect. "You'll have to excuse me," she said in a stilted voice. "I feel very queasy. I'm not used to this *rich* food!"

Olivia laid down her knife and fork, looking acutely distressed. "I'm so sorry, Dianne. It could only be the sauce. I kept the meal light."

"The food is delicious, Liv," Marsh assured her. "Not rich at all." In fact it was simple and elegant, the delicate seafood entrée followed by tender lamb fillets with a selection of fresh vegetables. Olivia had even gone to the trouble of preparing a special dessert for Dianne, a light apricot soufflé, but it was obvious her efforts had failed to please.

"Would you like someone to go up with you, Di?" Marsh asked. "If you're not feeling well in the morning I'll have a doctor fly in."

"I don't need *anyone*!" Dianne insisted with a sharp jut of her chin. It was as if the late Lady Faulkner was standing there. "You all go ahead. You get on so well!" With that, for a queasy woman she stormed away.

"I'll see she's all right." Justine pushed back her chair. "Not that I can say a thing right these days. Being pregnant doesn't seem to suit Di at all."

They all remained fairly silent until Justine returned barely four minutes later. "She's fine!" she said, slipping into her chair. "You look upset, Mrs. Earnshaw. You needn't be. The meal is delicious just as Marsh said. Di's got a bee in her bonnet about something."

And we all know what it is, Roslyn thought bleakly.

They had coffee at the table and later retired to the drawing room where Marsh opened up the lid of the Steinway grand. It wasn't the first time Roslyn had played it since her return to Macumba but it was the first time since then she had approached it feeling so upset. Her own idea of allowing Marsh's sisters time to settle in now seemed to make no sense. She should have gone down to the airstrip with Marsh with an engagement ring firmly planted on her finger. It was apparent Marsh was losing patience with the situation. Nevertheless the expression in his eyes as she walked to the piano found an answering chord in her.

"'The Lover and the Nightingale'. For *me*."

"Lovely!" Harry took a chair close to Olivia. He tipped his head back and closed his eyes, an expression of pleasure and expectancy on his face. Harry was a connoisseur.

From the moment her fingers touched the keys, Roslyn felt her agitation drain away. Her role was to interpret Granados' famous piece. She liked to think the composers were speaking to her. Sometimes she imagined she could almost see their faces. In her short life she had known tragedy, suffering and abandonment. Her playing, always technically secure, had developed considerable depth. A singing soul that spoke, like the nightingale, to the listener.

She played without interruption for perhaps forty minutes. The Spanish music she loved, several pieces from the Suite Española by Albeniz, on to Debussy's arabesques, ending with one of Harry's favourites, the beautiful D Flat Major nocturne by Chopin.

There was complete silence for a moment, a tribute to the spell, then Justine exclaimed, "It must be wonderful to feel so passionately about something! I enjoyed that immensely, Roslyn. One of your children at least should be so gifted.''

"I'll drink to that!" Marsh lifted his brandy goblet and drained it.

While Harry chose to remain with Olivia, Justine decided to accompany Marsh and Roslyn on their after dinner stroll. The night sky above Macumba was enthralling. The stars shone with great brilliance and luminosity, leading Roslyn to recount some of the myths and legends she had learned from Leelya in her childhood. She had just finished a story about the Morning Star when Justine said quite seriously, "You should really write all of this down. Our aboriginal people themselves will be pleased. I'm unhappy now to think we had nothing to do with Leelya or indeed any of the tribal people who regularly crossed the station. Yet Leelya saw you, Roslyn, a white child, as some sort of kindred spirit.''

"And I was honoured." Roslyn looked up, tracing the outstanding constellation of the Southern Cross. "I wonder what has happened to her."

"I'd say she's joined her ancestors up there." Marsh pointed to the glittering river of the Milky Way. "She would have been a great age. I'll make more inquiries. One of the boys came back with the story she was walking in the hill country. That was many months ago. Other women were with her. She could have been walking to the spot she wanted to die. Something to do with her dreaming.''

"If that's right, I know the spot," Roslyn said. "It's where she believed the rainbow touched the earth."

They parted in perfect harmony shortly before eleven, Roslyn and Justine to go to bed, Marsh to do a little more paperwork in the study.

"Listen, Ros, why don't we go riding tomorrow?" Justine suggested as they parted company in the upstairs gallery.

Roslyn thought swiftly. She treasured her early morning ride with Marsh, but Justine was showing the first signs of friendship. It was too important to be ignored. "Why not first thing in the morning, Justine, if you won't be too tired? It's the coolest part of the day."

"Oh, I can make it." Justine's attractive smile softened the angularity of her face. "Do you think Marsh would join us?"

"I can guarantee it," Roslyn said. "A six o'clock start?"

"Fine!" Justine turned back, bent on healing wounds. "Friends, Ros? How about it?"

On an impulse Roslyn went forward and embraced her. "It's what I've always wanted."

"Me, too. For years. We weren't very nice to you, were we?"

"You were awful. Just awful."

Justine winced. "But Marsh took care of you. He was crazy about you at one time."

"We were crazy together."

"Want to hear something to your advantage?" Justine looked directly into Roslyn's eyes. "He hasn't found anyone else."

It was a buoyant Roslyn who continued on to the room where she found her mother sitting quietly.

"What's up, Mumma?" Olivia's face wore a perturbed expression.

"Sit down, darling. There's something we have to talk about."

"Is it Dianne?" Roslyn asked anxiously. "I thought she'd gone to bed?"

"It's something Dianne *said*." Olivia suddenly slumped forward and rested her face in her hands. "Marsh cut her off, but I don't know for how long. Better I tell you myself."

Something in Roslyn seemed to snap. "Come on, Mumma. Get it out!"

"It's about your piano tuition," Olivia said, looking around her dully.

"Of course it is!" Roslyn threw herself on the bed. "The Faulkners paid for it."

Olivia shrugged forlornly. "Dame Agatha paid for it. It was something she wanted to do. She wanted to do it quietly. She believed you had a gift and she wanted to see it developed." Olivia glanced towards her daughter, who, instead of looking grateful, was alight with outrage. "Justine spoke tonight about her own family's musical abilities. I could have mentioned my own mother played the piano quite beautifully. She taught me up until the time she died. I never had the heart to touch the piano after that. My father couldn't bear to listen to me, either. *I* knew before Dame Agatha you had perfect pitch. But what could your father and I do? It was going to take all we had to send you away to school."

"For God's sake, Mumma, why didn't you tell me?"

Olivia looked mutely at her daughter for a moment. "You'd never have accepted the situation," she said finally. "You'd have rejected Dame Agatha's offer. You wouldn't be able to play today. Think of that!"

"And they all know?" Roslyn felt the sting of humiliation in her throat.

"Charles knew," Olivia said in a guarded voice. "He may have told Marsh later on. I'm certain neither of them would have told the girls, let alone Lady Faulkner. They were painfully aware of their resentments. They wouldn't have wanted to add to them."

"That's all very well, but Di knows now. That's what she was getting at. I thought it was odd."

"What's odd is how she's turning into her mother!" Olivia said sharply. "I would have thought marriage and the prospect of motherhood might make her mature, softer, more tolerant. Justine seems to have managed it, but Di has that same cutting way as her mother."

"What else did they pay for?" Roslyn asked. There was more. She could tell.

"Nothing. Until your father died. I did the best I could. Charles made up the rest. He loved you."

"He loved *you*, Mumma!" Roslyn sprang up from the bed, a whirlwind opening up a floodgate of memories in her mother. Roslyn at all stages. Up in arms. Fighting the hurts.

"Please don't upset yourself, darling," Olivia begged. "Maybe he did. Maybe he even said it. *Once*. We both had our honour. We'd made our commitments. If you're wondering about your piano, I paid for that entirely out of my own money."

"Oh, Mumma," Roslyn moaned, distressed.

"You worked very hard to help put yourself through university. I know what a grind it was. If I was forced to accept a helping hand, it was for your sake, Rosa. You weren't an ordinary child. Your father was thrilled with his little girl. Charles used to say you were like a precious stone. You had to be polished. It would have been a crime not to."

"And in all these years Marsh hasn't spoken one word of it to me."

"Surely you don't blame him?" Olivia was a little frightened of something in Roslyn's tone. "Marsh protected you as much as I did."

"We were bought. Both of us, Faulkner possessions."

Olivia looked stabbed to the heart. "What a way of putting it, Rosa. You always were overly dramatic. It was not bought. I was alone, vulnerable, in need of help. The Faulkners have a big philanthropic program in place. They offer several scholarships to gifted young people. Think of yourself as having received one."

"Not from the Faulkners!" Roslyn said.

"So this is what I get for speaking out? Next time I'll shut my mouth. You have to resolve your ongoing feud with this family, Rosa. What chance have you and Marsh got with this love-hate?"

"Maybe no chance at all!" Roslyn picked up a cushion and threw it.

"You're overreacting, Rosa." Olivia picked up the cushion and laid her aching head against it. "It was Dame Agatha's wish to remain anonymous."

"You mean she knew I suffered from the sin of pride?"

"Rosa, darling, we all knew that. Even Lady Faulkner couldn't break your spirit and she tried. Don't throw Dame Agatha's kindness and generosity in her face. She meant only good to come of this, as did Charles. Neither of them wanted you to feel under any obligation."

"I can't see how that's possible. I *do*."

CHAPTER SIX

ROSLYN waited just long enough for her mother to retire before she found her way downstairs again to the study. She realised she was in an emotional, excitable mood, but she was driven to have this issue out with Marsh. She felt anger, disillusionment, pain and, above all, *pity* for her mother's lack of power and position in life. Her father's early tragic death had forced them into a life of dependency. She *hated* it. She had always hated it. She could never get rid of the inner distress however good her intentions. In a way she identified too much with her mother. It couldn't be an uncommon situation with a lone parent and lone child. Maybe she had even assumed her father's role. She had certainly tried to fight her mother's battles, impose *her* nature on her gentler mother, but she had never succeeded in inciting her mother to revolt. Her mother's love for Charles Faulkner had been the crucial factor in their staying on at Macumba. Not that she could blame her mother for anything, but Olivia's decision had forced them into living under the power and protection of the family she had once called the Enemy. Maybe things would have been better for her had she not been such a bright child. She couldn't remember a time she hadn't wanted to better herself, intellectually, socially. She had spent all her school years *striving*. She had longed to be considered an equal by the Faulkner girls, covering her frustrations with a quick, ironic wit they couldn't match. As for

Marsh? Marsh was in her blood. Whether marriage was going to set all the wrongs right was another matter.

She rapped on the door of the study, opening it before he had a chance to respond.

"Rosa, my love!" He laid down his pen, his blue eyes embracing her. "One of these nights I'm going to put you in my pocket and take you up to bed."

"Can we talk?" She crossed the room so swiftly the skirt of her rose-printed chiffon dress swirled around her.

"Damn! I thought you'd come back to kiss me good-night." He rose from behind the desk and came round to her, his long arm gathering her up.

"Don't treat me with amusement," she warned him, tilting her dark head.

"Oh, my God, here we go again!" he said on a slow breath. "What is it this time, rosebud?"

"All these *years* and you've never told me."

"Ah, here it comes!"

"At least you're not going to pretend you don't know."

He released her and sat back on the desk. "All this melodrama, Rosa? There's nothing so terrible about it, is there? I assume you're talking about your piano lessons?"

"I am."

His sapphire eyes rested on her passionate face. "It wasn't Di. It must have been someone else."

"Not one of your precious sisters. Mumma told me. She was waiting for me in my room."

"Poor Liv!" He laughed shortly. "She's got one scary daughter!"

"What a thing to say, and you want to marry me?"

"I didn't say *I* was scared of you, Rosa. You've met your match. Which doesn't mean I'm not expecting lots of crisis situations. So Aggie paid for your piano lessons? Don't read anything indebted into it. Aggie could afford it and your parents couldn't."

"I should have been *told*!"

"I'm inclined to agree, but all in all we were locked into an explosive household."

"You mean, your mother's reaction?"

"She would have used it, Rosa."

She sank her teeth in her full, bottom lip. "Yes, she would. Let's get to how your *father* subsidized my education."

His expression assumed an arrogant cast. "Your mother was all alone in the world. She had no family in this country. No one outside of her friend, Ruth, to care about what happened to her. What did you think my father was going to do? Your father was killed in our employ. My father acted out of kindness and sympathy. Not that you were a charming kid, except when you felt like it, and then you could curl us both around your little finger. You had more prickles than a spiny anteater."

"I had to grow them for protection."

"You're just spoiling for a fight, aren't you?" He put out his hand and laid it along her cheek.

"Why didn't *you* tell me, Marsh? There was a time you could have told me anything and I would have accepted it."

"Unhappily in the past tense." His expression tautened. "For a long time I didn't *know*. My father didn't tell me everything. It was a private arrangement with your mother. You had to be given every chance. Helping you made him happy."

Her brilliant eyes flashed upwards. Her tone was hard and steady. "Are you sure it wasn't to get Mumma to sleep with him?"

"*Don't!*" he said grimly.

"What do we really know what went on?"

"They had their honour."

"So Mumma says."

"Then why don't you accept it?"

"You can't know what it's been like growing up. I love my mother, but I was never stupid. She wasted her life on an impossible dream. It's all so sad I want to scream."

"Then go ahead!" He pulled her to him roughly, his nostrils flaring, a disturbing curve to his mouth. "Scream if you have to, only let it *out!*"

It seemed like an invitation she couldn't resist. A therapeutic answer to the pressure points that plagued her. Her hands made fists. She pounded them against his hard, muscled chest.

"I hate you, Marsh," she gritted, which of course was nonsense. Without Marsh she was half a person but she was awash with emotions Dianne's arrival had set loose.

It was as if a whip had flicked him, raising weals on his flesh. "Maybe you have a right!"

The light gleamed queerly across his bronzed cheek-bones, darkened his eyes to an electric blue-violet. For a time he tolerated her pent-up railing, then he grew tired of it, bringing her fists together and holding them still. "It's *loving* you want," he said thickly. "Loving until you can't remember the hurt."

Even as his face swam above her, Roslyn started to shudder. She made a grab for his arm, but he bent her body back in a supple arc, seeking the magenta shadow at the base of her low, scoop-necked dress, moving lower over the sinuous chiffon so her flesh beneath its thin covering *burned*.

Sensation upon sensation was moving through her like ever-widening ripples on a lake. There was so much between them; their shared history, their passionate loving, the deep resentments that suddenly flared up and set them on a collision course. Passion and sexual hostility was so intermingled it was impossible to say where it was coming from.

She gasped as he allowed her up, turning his questing mouth on hers. Her soft lips opened in overwhelming longing. Their tongues curled, mated, until it became such a pressure they had to break off to breathe deeply, then return to the intense sensual exploration that doubled the excitement with every frantic moment....

Marsh grasped a handful of her glistening hair, stared hard into her eyes. "Sleep with me, Rosa. Now, tonight!"

As if it hadn't been her fantasy more times than she could possibly count! Yet she said in a kind of desperate rush, "We go up to your bedroom just like that?"

He looked at her searchingly. "You're ready. Do you think I don't know that?"

"Always ready for you. That's no secret."

"A rosebud under spring rain." He ran his finger around the outline of her full lips. "I can't take this waiting, Rosa. I'm a man, with all a man's needs!"

"Then you must try discipline." She shook her head. "I can't...I won't sleep with you until I'm your wife!"

For a moment he looked at her, blue fire in his eyes, then he laughed, self-derision etched into the little brackets around his mouth.

"Them's fightin' words, Rosa," he drawled. "I don't know that you're going to be able to pull it off."

"We had a bargain."

"Did we now! I said nothing about total abstinence. I'm *starved* for what we had. In fact I think I'm heading for some sort of crackup."

"Not you, Marsh. You forgot me for years."

His beautiful mouth twisted in a smile. "I thought that was what you wanted. You couldn't tell me enough you'd stopped loving me."

"Love wasn't enough!"

"You wanted marriage. Well, you've got it. So why make it sound as if there's a big question hanging over the whole thing?"

"It's my suspicious nature. You'll have to pardon it."

"More like you want to turn me inside out."

"Whatever it takes! I've learned the hard way it's much better to play hard to get. *You* taught me that."

He caught her hand, carried it to his mouth. "You're a cruel little cat, which makes me wonder why I want you. I could think of at least a dozen women who wouldn't act this way. Kim Petersen included."

"I thought maybe you'd slept with her."

"Sleeping with a woman is easy. Loving her is an entirely different thing. It so happens I'm crazy about you. Emotions tend to obscure the mind. It was a terrible mistake letting you get away from me."

She put out her slender arms, rested them on his wide shoulders. "I'm amazed it wasn't forever."

"Will you *ever* forgive me, Rosa?" There it was, the flash of vulnerability in the stunning self-assuredness.

She could have said no. Instead her extraordinary topaz eyes filled with tears. She didn't lift a finger to wipe them away. They gathered and fell, in shining crystal drops.

"Rosa...darling!" He drew her in utter tenderness against him, his sensitivity as always disarming her. "Why can't we end this futile war? We've been happy since your return, haven't we? So Dianne arrived to create a few problems. She's not behaving well. But I'm not going to let her get away with it for long. On the other hand, why don't we simply tell them we're getting married? The limbo has to end."

"Oh, I know, Marsh." She allowed him to gently dry her tears. "It's just that your family scramble me up so much."

"When will a wounded little girl accept her womanhood, her own worth?"

"When your family play fair."

"You have Justine's vote. That's a beginning. Frankly I don't think you need anyone's vote but mine and you have it overwhelmingly."

"I still won't sleep with you." She smiled. She was feeling so much better. Kisses were ravishing. Comfort was important.

His fine white teeth showed in an ironic grin. "I hope you don't fancy yourself as another Anne Boleyn?"

"Her end was too unattractive. How did Dianne get to know Dame Agatha paid for my piano lessons?"

Marsh shrugged. "You know what an avid eavesdropper she was as a girl. Aggie would never have told her. Nor Dad. I certainly didn't. Does her knowing bother you so much?"

"In a way it seems to undermine my self-value. Maybe I wouldn't feel like that if Dianne wasn't so unkind."

"Then someone has to tell her. That someone is me!"

"She'd see it as a betrayal. I don't want you to say anything unless it all gets too intense. I should be fighting my own battles. A line has to be drawn somewhere with

Di. You realise why she jumped up from the table? She was furious Mumma was sitting down with us.''

"That makes her look an appalling snob. I can't defend her. On the other hand, don't let it get to you. It's Dianne who has to iron out that particular unattractive kink. It sure as hell would help if you and I got engaged before Chris gets here. Married or not, you're the sort of woman he loses his cool over.''

"And I'm a total innocent!'' Roslyn frowned at the prospect. "As far as I'm concerned, Chris is a—''

"Don't say it!'' Marsh begged, holding up two palms.

"Lord knows I was only going to say 'twit.'''

"Whatever. You can handle it.''

"Of course. The one I can't handle is *you*.'' She leaned closer and pressed a butterfly kiss on his mouth.

The girls were scarcely home before Kim Petersen flew over, piloting her own single-engined Cessna, a birthday present from her father.

"I thought I might stay a day or two,'' she announced unnecessarily. Down in the driveway Ernie was bow-legged under the weight of her two suitcases.

"That will be lovely!'' Dianne looked overjoyed to see her. "I've missed you so much!'' She threw her arms around her friend, kissing her Euro-style.

"Good to see you, Kim!'' Justine smiled in turn, swishing cheeks. "Roslyn is here to join us.'' She turned to include Roslyn in the group.

"Yes, I *know*. How are you, Roslyn?'' Kim's large grey-green eyes examined Roslyn from head to toe. Kim was as tall as her friends, but far better looking. Her sun-streaked, dark blond hair was precision cut to swing in a thick, medium-length pageboy. Her clear, tanned skin was innocent of make-up, except for a natural, dark pink lip gloss. Her ultra-slim body, fit and tightly muscled was encased in a white linen shirt and matching wide-legged pants, stylish leather sandals on her feet, a handsome leather belt around her trim waist. She looked what she was. A rich young woman, super confident and competent. Unlike Marsh's sisters, she had always taken a deep interest and active part in the running of her father's cattle and sheep chain.

"I'm very well, Kim. And you?" Roslyn went forward, prepared to take Kim's hand, but it wasn't offered.

"Couldn't be better!" The tanned face smiled, but the eyes held their familiar condescension.

"Why don't I show you up to your room?" Dianne was quite pink with pleasure. "It's not your usual one. For some reason Roslyn's got that, but we've prepared another."

Just as Roslyn thought. It had all been arranged.

"Any other changes I should know about?" Kim laughed as she and Dianne walked from the veranda into the cool of the spacious entrance hall.

"I'll go, too. See she's settled." Justine turned a vaguely apologetic face to Roslyn. "It's nice to have Kim here. We've always been great friends."

"Yes, I know." Roslyn smiled, but a kind of sadness moved through her. She would never be accepted in this multi-layered world, where friendships went back generations. Better get used to it, she thought. Cultivate your own inner strengths. Build your own dynasty if you have to.

Fifteen minutes later all three young women returned to the veranda where Roslyn was still sitting. She had committed herself to a course of action. She was prepared to see it through.

"Still here, Ros?" Kim asked casually, as though Roslyn might have sought refuge in the kitchen.

"I hope that's okay?"

"But of course!" Justine sounded dismayed.

Dianne, however, settled herself back comfortably in a planter's chair.

"Still suffering morning sickness, are you, poor angel?" Kim flopped rather gracelessly into a wicker armchair facing her.

"Strangely enough not for the past two days. It must be something in Macumba's air. The purity and the wonderful, comforting scents." Dianne glanced across at Roslyn, still wearing the elegant riding clothes that became her so well. "Ros, do you think you could ask your mother to bring coffee and tea out here?"

Justine immediately jumped up. "Don't worry, Ros. I'm going back inside for a minute. I'll ask."

Kim looked hugely surprised. "In that case, stay and talk to us," she invited. "I've got to hand it to you, you've certainly got yourself together. You look marvellous. So what brings you back to Macumba? You haven't been here for a couple of years surely?"

Roslyn adjusted her chair so she could join the circle. "Mumma, of course. Then Marsh wanted me to be here." She held Kim's faintly scornful glance unwaveringly, watching it dissipate into ludicrous shock.

"*Marsh*?" Both young women cried out together, making it almost a shout.

"You sound surprised?" Roslyn kept her expression cool and polite.

"Well, *I* am, dear." Kim ran a strong hand through her thick fall of hair. "Considering Marsh never *once* mentioned you."

"You wouldn't have been all that interested in news of me, would you, Kim?"

Kim lifted a linen clad knee then stamped one of her sandals on the floor, rather like a horse. "I certainly would! I don't want anyone trying to muscle in on my man. And that includes you, young Earnshaw. Not that you'd be in the running," she added in her insulting fashion.

"Is that a joke?" Roslyn asked.

"Joke?" Kim looked at the younger Roslyn as though she'd gone temporarily mad. "It's a plain statement of fact."

"As *you* see it?"

"I'll say!" Kim looked to Dianne for confirmation and support.

"Then forgive me if I take exception to the implications. You have an embarrassingly large ego. As far as I'm concerned, we're all equal."

Kim eyed her contemptuously. "Come off it, Ros. I have a pedigree. Surely you don't expect me not to take pride in it?"

"You're a horsewoman. You know pedigree is secondary to performance. Call it character if you like. Distinguished people are generally egalitarian."

"It is dreadfully hot," Dianne suddenly said.

"Give your mother a shout," Kim told Roslyn firmly.

"She'll be here presently. Would you like a fan, Di?"

"I'd like you two to stop scrapping at one another."

"I'm sorry," Roslyn apologised. "I don't want any unpleasantness, either, but I can't sit quietly while Kim makes me the target for her somewhat brutal put-downs. I endured too much of that in the past. Now I want things to be different. I'd be glad of a little civility, not this absurd pulling rank. Take it from me, the Colonial era has passed."

"So the word's got around?" Kim barely controlled a supercilious smirk.

"After many discouraging setbacks. Please remember I'm here as Marsh's guest. Maybe a great deal more."

There, she'd almost put it in a nutshell!

As a consequence Dianne gave a little cry of alarm and Kim braced herself as though for battle. "Now you've got us utterly befuddled. What do you *mean*, exactly?"

"I mean, the situation has changed," Roslyn said calmly.

"Interesting!" Kim said grimly. "I had the feeling you were up to something."

"So you lost no time in flying over?"

"My dear, I had advance warning."

"She means *me*!" Dianne looked as though she suddenly detested herself.

"The fact you've always had a thing going with Marsh hasn't bypassed us entirely," Kim said with an insolent lift of her brows. "You *are* beautiful in a cloying sort of way."

Dianne looked thoroughly startled. "Cloying?" she blurted. "Is that what you'd say of a bouquet of red roses? I've always wanted to look like Ros. Naturally I loathed her when I didn't. I still haven't learned to live with it."

"Dearest, what the devil are you babbling about?" Kim cried.

"It's this pregnancy," Dianne laughed weakly. "I wish it would get a move on. Ros, do you think you could be a pal and give your mother a call? You've no idea how I'm longing for a cup of tea."

"No problem!" Roslyn responded. And it wasn't, put like that.

"It's fairly obvious your mother has got a bit slack," Kim began severely, but was interrupted by the sound of the trolley being wheeled through the hallway.

Roslyn stood up immediately trying to control her quick temper, but it was Justine who eventually appeared. "Sorry about the delay." She pushed the trolley forwards, her expression positively chirpy. "Poor old Harry cut his hand and Mrs. E. had to dress it. God, it was harrowing! Blood everywhere!"

"Do you *mind*?" The freckles stood out on Dianne's pale skin.

"Sorry, old dear!" Justine gave her sister an apologetic smile. "It looked worse than it was. Mrs. E. dealt with it very efficiently."

"If that's what it takes to make you happy!" Dianne said.

"I'm not telling you *all* I know."

"Obviously you're going to make us wait for it," Kim said, accepting a cup of coffee from Justine while Roslyn attended to Dianne's lemon tea.

"Will you look at these scones!" Justine cried. "I've never been able to make a decent scone in my life. They're supposed to be so *easy*!"

"*Well*?" Dianne looked at her sister fretfully.

Justine sat down. Arranged herself comfortably. "Prepare yourselves for an astonishing tidbit."

"Has it anything to do with Ros?" Kim asked sharply.

Justine shook her tawny head. "Harry cut himself because he's in a state of shock. It appears he stands to inherit a baronetcy. And a stately pile. Some ancient relative of his is dying in England. Lord Marchmont, Mortimer, something like that."

"Good Lord!" Kim sat erect in her chair. "To tell you the truth, I'm not surprised. Harry has always handled himself in the grand manner."

"He put plain old 'gardener' on his income tax return," Roslyn pointed out mildly. "When did he find out?"

"The news was waiting for him this morning. Faxed to him by one of his sons. He has to return home."

"You mean, he's going to take it up?" Dianne asked eagerly.

"First things first, Di. The old gent has to die. Harry was very fond of him apparently."

"He must have known he was the heir, surely?" Roslyn asked.

"You'll have to ask your mother," Justine responded in an arch voice. "She was the first to know. In fact I wouldn't be a bit surprised if Harry didn't ask her to marry him now."

"Why on earth would you say that?" Dianne looked at her sister sharply to see if she was ribbing them.

"God, you're dense sometimes, Di. Harry's been in love with Mrs. E. for as long as I can remember. Don't you agree, Ros?"

"I think that's what's kept him hanging in."

"You mean, on the station?" Dianne demanded.

"Yes."

"But he'll be a baronet now," Dianne said stonily.

"I wish I knew what you're getting at." Roslyn's topaz eyes started to blaze.

"They don't come more patrician-looking than Mrs. E." Justine said supportively, and touched Roslyn's arm. "So in a little while we'll have a lord in our midst, or Harry won't come back at all."

While the others stayed on the veranda discussing the matter and reminiscing about old times in which Harry largely figured, Roslyn wheeled the trolley back into the kitchen where she found her mother and Harry sitting at the table, drinking coffee, their expressions engrossed.

"So, m'lord, how are you?" Roslyn asked with gentle mockery, looking at his bandaged hand.

Harry turned his kindly face towards her. "Plain shell-shocked, darlin'. Justine told you, obviously?"

"Yes."

"I would have liked to tell you myself only she happened to walk in at a crucial time."

"That's all right, Harry."

"Come and sit down. Join us in our little talk."

"Harry has asked me to marry him," Olivia said, looking at her daughter with half-rueful, half-sparkling eyes.

"What a one he is!" Roslyn put her hands on Harry's shoulders and kissed his cheek. "Taking all things into account, I'm happy to give you my blessing."

"She hasn't accepted me yet, duckie." Harry laughed.

"I haven't said no, either." Olivia smiled. "I want time to think this over, Harry."

"What, another ten years?" he crowed. "No, no, m'love, it's not on. It's now or never!"

"That's it, Harry. Sweep her off her feet."

"It's such a big decision," Olivia said. "I'm not good at making decisions."

"You can say that again!" Harry sighed, his expression turning a little bleak. "Faulkner was a dream, Liv. Nothing could ever have come of it. Now he's gone."

"Harry!" Olivia looked stricken. "Why would you speak of Charles now. And in front of Rosa?"

"Because she knows better than anyone else," he answered in a quiet but blunt voice. "You have to lay your ghost to rest, Liv. *I* love you. I have from the moment I set eyes on you. I've stayed on Macumba to be near you, now it's time to take up my own heritage."

"Then you'll want to stay in England, Harry?" Roslyn asked.

"Oh, yes, m'dear. I love this country. It's young and vigorous and it's been kind to me, but England is where my roots are. That's where I want to die."

"I understand that, Harry," Roslyn told him, "but you'd be taking Mumma away from me."

"Nonsense!" Harry reached across the table and patted Roslyn's hand. "Liv's told me you and Marsh are to marry. Don't worry, your news is safe with me. I'm absolutely delighted for you both. In my opinion you're splendidly matched. But when you're married, you'll need to be on your own. If your mother honours me by accepting my proposal I'll take her back to England with me, yes. She *is* English lest we all forget. But we would expect you and Marsh to visit us frequently. At the very least, once a year. That should present no problems. Marsh travels a great deal as it is. He has relatives of his own in England. He visits them all the time."

"But Harry—" Olivia said.

"No buts, darling," he interrupted forcefully. "I'm certain in my heart we could be very happy. You care for me a good deal more than you've been prepared to acknowledge. Who was frantic when I came a cropper at our last polo match?"

"I think you should stop playing polo," Olivia said. "You've had a pretty good run."

"I promise to stop if you promise to marry me." Harry caught Olivia's hand and carried it to his lips. "Think of it as saving my life."

The following morning Marsh flew Harry to the nearest domestic airport where he was booked on a flight to Brisbane, the state capital, which in turn hooked up with a Qantas flight direct to London. Roslyn and Olivia went along for the first leg of the trip, hugging Harry warmly before he was forced to obey the final boarding call.

"Love you, love you!" he called, an unfamiliar figure in a beautifully tailored city suit.

"Why do I have the feeling Harry's proposed?" Marsh glanced over to where Olivia was standing so demurely, waving a silk scarf.

"I wanted to tell you but Mumma hasn't given him her answer yet," Roslyn explained.

"*That* doesn't surprise me," Marsh said dryly.

"I think she loves him." Roslyn's voice trailed away.

"I think she *could* if she gave herself half a chance. They're very good friends. As far as I'm concerned that's a lot!"

"I remember when *we* used to be very good friends."

"I remember, too." He looked down at her, the expression in his sapphire eyes setting up a faint tremble.

In the near distance the jet turned in preparation for the taxi down the runway. "Oh, I do hope he'll be all right!" Olivia moved over to join them, her gentle face anxious. "Such a long, long trip! He'll be exhausted, poor darling."

Marsh gave a casual shrug. "Harry's tough, in excellent condition. I just hope he makes it in time."

"I don't believe what's happening around here anymore," Olivia said in a bemused voice. "You and Rosa to be married. Now Harry wants to marry me." She tilted her head, looking directly into Marsh's eyes.

"Why are you looking at me like that, Liv?" he demanded. "Do you want *my* permission? You've got it. You and Harry are family. I could easily learn to call you Lady Mortimer," he teased.

Olivia didn't smile. She continued to stare up into his striking face with its strong echoes of his father's vivid blue eyes, firm jaw and cleanly defined mouth. "You're so much like your father," she said. "It's impossible to forget him with you around."

To Roslyn it was the most revealing thing her mother had ever said. Marsh must have thought so, too, because he looked down at Olivia in silence for a moment before he answered. "Dad would have approved, Liv. You need a great deal more out of life. In a sense you've been hiding away. I've been very grateful, but it's not what you deserve. Harry is a fine man. When he first came to us he was teetering on the edge of emotional collapse. Macumba took him in, allowed him to heal. His problem of recent times has been getting you to marry him. You must realise he truly loves you?"

"Oh, I *do*!" Olivia looked agonised. "I've done everything but face it. Goodness knows why. I love him, too, as a person. I'm terribly upset he's going away. I'd be devastated if I thought I'd never see him again, it's just . . . it's just . . ."

"No explanation to offer?" Marsh prompted gently.

"No explanation I can offer." Olivia's beautiful eyes filled with tears.

Marsh put his arm around her shoulder and they all began to walk on. "It's all got to do with dreams, Liv," he said. "We all have our dreams but it's not always the way life *is*. Harry can give you a good life. At the same time you can make him whole. It seems to me you'll be making a big mistake if you lose him.''

''Do you think I could?'' Olivia sounded shaken.

''This inheritance thing has forced the issue. Harry's not the man to give up easily but he will expect an answer.''

Olivia gave a ragged little laugh. ''When you put it like that, Marsh, I've a strong urge to step on a plane.''

''Well, now,'' said Marsh. ''Just say the word.''

CHAPTER SEVEN

ROSLYN sat her horse in the shade of a silvery coolibah looking down on the spectacle of brumby running on the quivering plain below. The ridge was a wonderful vantage point—she was sharing it with two inquisitive kangaroos—but the glare was harsh. It did funny things to the landscape, making it seem to swim in shimmering heat waves. She crammed her Akubra further down on her head, tilting the brim against the shattering brilliance that pierced the light, leafy canopy. Burning ochre dust, the vivid Namatjira red, rose in a great cloud as some fifty brumbies were being driven towards the holding yard at Inga-warri. Inga-warri was an old camping ground and the horses could water there at the large dam.

She waved to the kangaroos who looked at one another then appeared to nod at her gravely. She knew kangaroos could be a terrible menace but they had always charmed her. There were countless aboriginal myths and legends about the travels of Kangaroo and Euro on their journeys through central Australia. They were mythical creatures and there was no question they could look, like now, extraordinarily dignified. Interesting, too, they weren't in the least unsettled by her presence or the ear-splitting noise that came from the plain.

In the old days running and yarding wild horses was considered the greatest of sports. She'd had a lot of fun herself but of recent times motorbikes were being utilised on Macumba to capture the plentiful mobs just as the helicopter was used on the musters. Now the silent plain was split by the spine-tingling roar of four Yamaha 600 cc's herding the bush horses. It was exciting but very dangerous work, especially in the scrub. Sometimes the stallion fearing for his mares would try to savage a rider. The slightest mistake with the bike and the rider could and often did end up in hospital.

"Lucky" Redding, so called because everyone said he was lucky he wasn't dead, had crashed four times in the last eighteen months. Twice on Macumba when the Royal Flying Doctor had to be called in to rescue him. "Lucky" was out there today in hot pursuit of the big bay buck stallion. Roslyn hoped he was wearing his lucky talisman, a roughly star-shaped stone a part-aboriginal friend had picked up on one of his ritual walkabouts in the gibber desert with its vast pavement of sparkling coloured stones. Roslyn had dozens of them Marsh had helped her collect as a child. The gibber plains are remarkable phenomena, the stones rounded and polished by windblown sand until they resemble gemstones. Lying embedded in the ochred clays, they resemble a fantastic glazed mosaic. "Lucky's" talisman was a curious semi-transparent quartz with a marking like an Egyptian hieroglyphic in the centre. A spirit stone Lucky's friend had called it. It seemed to work, though not totally.

The dust was rising now in a turning, twisting cumulus cloud, blown up by a sudden hot wind that seemed to come out of nowhere, the willy-willies that were supposed to be sent as a warning. The horses appeared to be in superb condition. Their muscles rippled in the dazzling light, coats taut against their lean frames. The stallion appeared to have a lot of Thoroughbred in him. His ancestor had probably escaped from the station at some stage. There were more than half a million wild horses in Australia. This mob looked a fine lot. The bikkies had been on the go since dawn. As far as she knew they were to cover the northwestern corner ranging over a few hundred kilometres. They would stop soon for smoko. She wouldn't say no to a cup of billy tea herself. Marsh had a meeting going with an important horse breeder. She had left Kim and the girls lazing the time away beside the pool. Justine had invited her to join them in her new, friendly fashion, but she had taken pity on the glance Kim and Dianne had exchanged. She was feeling much better in herself now. Stronger. When it was all said and done, the only person who really mattered was Marsh. Let the others think what they liked.

As she commenced her descent of the rolling, stony slope, Roslyn saw some of the horses make a break, while the others cunningly bolted in the opposite direction. She held her breath, but within minutes Lucky and his team had wheeled them in. Men on horseback would have had little chance against this lot, she thought. They would have been outrun. The horses were wonderfully fit. They were on their own territory. They knew every inch of the scrub.

She made it into camp at the same time the weary mob were being driven by the tailers, the stockmen on horses, who shepherded the subdued brumbies into a temporary holding yard. The stallion was still looking unpredictable but the bikes were ready to wheel him back into the tailers who were handling them with the ease of long experience.

"Hi, Ros!" Tall, blond, laconic Lucky parked his powerful Yamaha then removed his helmet. His face and clothes were covered in bright red dust that he cheerfully brushed and thumped off. "That was some chase. Hard work."

"At least you're in one piece." She dismounted and tethered her horse, responding with a smile and a wave to the rest of the work party.

"Wearin' m'lucky charm, that's why." He limped over, favouring his gammy leg, courtesy of an 80 m.p.h. flight through the fork of a tree. "So where's the boss?" he asked, easing himself down onto a convenient tree stump.

"He had a meeting. What about a cup of billy tea? That should go down well?"

"Wouldn't even touch the sides!" Lucky turned his tousled, white-gold head. "Blackie," he yelled. "Get the billy on, will ya? Ros wants a cup of tea. The blokes will want one, as well."

"Gotcha!" Blackie bellowed back, making Roslyn think the day-in, day-out roar of the bikes might be making them a little deaf.

"So, long time no see. Tell me what you've been doin'?" Lucky invited. "I don't mean to be cheeky like, but is it possible you're even more beautiful?"

Roslyn sat back, meeting the twinkling gaze. "Come off it, Lucky! You're seeing me through rose-coloured dust."

"I'll be damned if I am." Lucky grinned.

They were all relaxing over their second cup of tea when Marsh drove the Jeep into camp. He had someone with him.

"Well, if it ain't the high-and-mighty Miss Petersen!" Lucky muttered beneath his breath. "Just watch 'er give us the big ignore."

In fact Kim condescended to give them all a regal wave, but chose to remain within the safe confines of the Jeep.

"Who does she think she is, the bloody Queen?" Lucky groaned, and struggled to his feet.

"You couldn't ask for a better wave than that, Lucky," Roslyn teased.

Marsh was crossing the short distance between them, easy and nonchalant, the most graceful male. He had swept the sides of his pearl-grey Akubra up but the front was tilted down rakishly over his eyes.

"Rosa, I thought I might find you here," he said. "How's it going, Lucky?" He lifted an arm in salute to the rest of the men who responded in kind.

"I've been watching the chase," Roslyn told him. "It was quite exciting!"

"I'll bet! The only thing that surprises me is you didn't join in."

"I can't ride the bike yet."

"And you're not going to," he said. "So don't let me catch you trying. Hear, Lucky?"

"Sure, Boss, but she's the gamest girl I ever came across."

"Just think of your own injuries, Lucky. How's the leg?"

Lucky looked down and grimaced. "I'm always amazed it's holdin' me up."

"You really ought to get out of the business." Marsh was frowning, looking towards the railed enclosure.

"I will when I'm thirty," Lucky promised. "Think you could find a job for me?"

"No problem." Marsh looked back. "We could do with another rail. I don't think it's high enough to accommodate the stallion. He's enormous for a brumby and too damned restless for my liking. It's astonishing what an animal like that can do. Some of them even love fences. Get onto it, Lucky."

"Sure, Boss!" Lucky limped away, yelling at his mate Blackie at the same time.

"I'll be damned if Lucky's not going deaf," Marsh said.

"Blackie, as well," Roslyn said ruefully. "You're right about that extra rail. Will you just look at the glare in the stallion's eye! 'Think you've beaten me! The devil you have!' Come to think of it, he's got a look of Blazer." She referred to a magnificent hunter Sir Charles had kept.

"You've got keen eyes, Rosa." Marsh nodded approvingly. "I was just thinking the same thing myself. Blazer got away once for at least half a day. This fellow could well be the produce of a bush mating. He's got Blazer's distinctive mark. Go and talk to Kim until we get the rail up."

"Could be she doesn't want to talk to me?"

Marsh smiled. "I've got to tell you she doesn't know what she's missing. Come back in the Jeep with us. One of the men can bring the mare in."

Roslyn took off her hat and let the breeze ruffle her neatly coiled hair. "Need protection?"

"One thing I've learned. Never, *ever*, trust a woman."

"Not when they've been flinging themselves at you since you were fourteen years old."

"Rosa, darling, more like fifteen," he said.

Kim's eyes surveyed her coolly as she approached the Jeep. "Do you think it's wise being one of the boys?"

"Why not? I find them chivalrous and friendly like most men in the bush."

"My father always says it's a mistake to come down to that level."

"But then, he was raised as an old feudal baron. Most of them have got out of the habit."

Kim shrugged. "Well, what you do with your time has nothing to do with me. I was just trying to give you a piece of advice, that's all. You're always *trying* to aim higher."

Roslyn looked at the other young woman thoughtfully. "Why are you always so rude to me? I mean, you really want to *hurt*."

"And you're the perfect target. I figure you're a threat." Kim smiled tightly. "I'm not telling you that to get your hopes up. It's more a warning."

Roslyn sighed. "Not another one!"

"You haven't had any for a *while*. I'm glad you decided to come over. I've been waiting to have a word with you. It's so difficult in front of Dianne and Justine."

"What is?" Roslyn swatted at a flying insect.

Kim stared at her with hard eyes. "What you think you're getting up to," she said finally.

"Any clues?" Roslyn's topaz eyes were shining in her spirited face.

"Don't waste time trying to be smart," Kim answered in an infuriated voice.

"But I *am* smart, Kim. I heard you never got your degree."

"I couldn't be bothered going on with it, that's why. I didn't need to go out and find myself a job."

"What a pity!" Roslyn said lightly. "You might have been all the better for a little struggle."

Kim laughed harshly, narrowing her eyes. "Look, this kind of banter leaves me cold. You say you're smart? Well, be smart enough not to interfere with *my* plans."

"You still won't give me any clues."

"So help me!" Kim pleaded to no one at all. "You know exactly what I'm talking about. I daresay Marsh isn't averse to tumbling you in the hay. You seem to have the patent on that femme fatale stuff. But you'll no more

get him to marry you than you were able to in the past.
All I can say is, you must really *love* punishment."

"And it seems to make *you* happy doling it out. Can't
you come up with something better than a tumble in the
hay? Marsh is as fastidious as hell."

"Oh, I know," Kim said softly. "So it's still going on
between you two?"

Roslyn glanced up as two brilliantly enamelled parrots
landed in a tree. "I don't think it ever stopped."

A ripple passed along Kim's long throat. "And you're
happy in the role of a little bit on the side?"

"Actually it's a role I wouldn't consider."

Kim pushed forward sharply in her seat, giving Roslyn
the impression Kim would have liked to strike her. Sad,
but not impossible. She even braced herself. "My dear,
that's how he treats you." Kim sneered.

"You could say that's how he's treated us both. Lift
a finger and we come running. Not that he isn't one
splendid prize, but I refuse to do it anymore."

"You surely can't think you can get him to marry
you?" Kim challenged, at the same time turning a little
white.

"I'm working on it." Roslyn shrugged.

"Then you're *mad*!" Kim said with a violent hiss. "I
mean, who would accept you? You'd be snubbed at every
turn."

"Hey, what's with you and the snobbery?" Roslyn's
own voice sharpened. "Only a fool would play that
game. Who'd take the risk of insulting Marsh Faulkner's
wife? Why would they want to? I may not have been
born into the establishment, but I'm a long way from
unacceptable. I'm young, well-educated, presentable. I
don't look like a camel in disguise, which has been said
of your friend Suzanne Crawley."

"Suzanne is a sweet girl," Kim said shortly. "She certainly wouldn't bother with someone like you. Isn't it enough for you Lady Faulkner *hated* you?"

"It was rare for Lady Faulkner to like *anyone*. She wasn't overfussed on her own daughters."

"I think she was disappointed they're so plain." Kim permitted herself the remark, then looked like she wished she hadn't said it. "Anyway, she liked me. She approved of me."

"Well it's doubtful she would have looked at someone who was destitute. It's possible she put you and your mother on the wrong track, too. You've put a lot of years and a lot of heartache into trying to land Marsh. It doesn't look like he wants to marry you, though, does it?"

"Look here, how dare you challenge me!" Kim said in a hard, angry voice. "Marsh and I are deeply involved. There are a lot of things you don't know."

"I know you might have been lovers at one time, but unfortunately for you, the allure wore off."

"Boy, have you got that wrong!" Kim retaliated, eyes flashing outrage.

"I don't think so," Roslyn said quietly. "This is a go-nowhere conversation. Why don't we wind it up?"

"On the contrary, I want to get to the bottom of this—" Kim broke off, startled as there was a loud crash close at hand. Roslyn, too, turned her head in alarm, pulling up her bandana against the spiralling cloud of thick dust. When it settled she saw the two stockmen making a desperate attempt to reposition the final top rail. The rest of the men were making a variety of calls, whistles, threats, trying to calm the horses, but it was obvious the stallion with its superior intelligence saw this as its chance for freedom.

It reared wildly, making a weird, screaming sound like a battle cry. The harem moved back respectfully at this spectacle of rearing male pride. Powerful hooves flailed the air then came down thunderously on the red sand. The wild horse backed up, then, while the men dived for cover, flew at the fence, soaring fully extended for a moment before it came down on the other side, unable momentarily to galvanise itself into a gallop.

With a frenzied, "Dear heavens!" Kim threw herself into the driver's seat, hitting the ignition and putting the Jeep into reverse. The swift violence of the action pitched Roslyn, who had been leaning against the Jeep, off balance. She went down hard, thinking fatalistically, *I'm going to die*. No time now to get out of harm's way. It was all happening in seconds. A warm body threw itself over her. *Lucky*.

"God Almighty, what a bastard!" he moaned, trying to drag them to some kind of safety, while his boots kept slipping in the sand. "This is it, luv!"

And it might have been only Marsh in his lightning way had sized up the situation putting himself right where he should be, in the saddle, spinning out a lasso that fell unerringly, miraculously, over the fleeting stallion's neck. It came up with a mighty jolt, in turn almost jerking Marsh out of the saddle. While they all looked on, helpless, he managed to right himself, adhering to the quiet, powerful quarter horse while the brumby reared and bucked frantically, hell-bent on unseating him and mauling the station workhorse.

"If that's not the most brilliant throw of the century, I'll eat my gloves!" Lucky yelled in Roslyn's ear. The brumby was careering madly in circles now, unable to break Marsh's domination. Had it been the time to appreciate it instead of lying half stunned with her heart in her mouth Roslyn would have found it a marvellous exhibition of skill and control. Finally the stallion was brought to stand with nothing more than a neck rope, man's authority and iron nerve.

"That's a classic!" Lucky whooped like a fan at a rodeo. "Ya not gunna see any better!"

"You're pretty fearless yourself, Lucky." Roslyn sat up gingerly. "I'm sorry you had to take a tumble trying to save me."

"You and me are mates," he told her cheerfully. "Besides, it was the boss who saved us. He's one daring guy. Rumour has it he'd put his life on the line for you anytime."

Roslyn looked at him in astonishment. "Where did you hear *that*?"

"Here and there!" Lucky answered with a grin. "He stopped that horse for ya. No mess, no fuss. Love's what me mum would call it. Here, let me help you up. What Miss Petersen done could be called all sorts of things, but love ain't one o'them."

"Self-preservation?" On her feet, Roslyn began to dust herself off.

"I think I'd use something stronger. Speak of the lady and here she comes. No doubt to explain the dastardly deed."

"I hope not." Roslyn didn't want to hear a word from Kim.

If Kim's sickly pallor was any indication, she wasn't altogether happy with her own actions. "Roslyn, are you all right?" she called, her voice full of anxiety and distress. "There was so little time. I just had to move the Jeep. You understand?"

Roslyn swung around nursing a skinned elbow. "Words fail me."

"I'm so shocked. I got such a fright."

"Couldn't you have yelled *stand clear*!"

"There wasn't time. We would have been trapped between a maddened wild animal and its freedom."

"I *was* trapped, Kim," Roslyn said simply. "In fact, Lucky and I would have been mush without Marsh's intervention."

"He's astonishing," Kim said tearfully. "He threw himself into terrible danger for us."

"Except you managed to get the Jeep thirty feet away. I think you would have kept on going only you backed yourself into a tree."

"At least credit me with quick thinking," Kim pleaded. "There was simply nothing I could do about you. I'm so dreadfully sorry."

"Bunkum!" Roslyn said pleasantly.

"I think I'll get Marsh to take me back to the house." Kim fished out a handkerchief from her pant's pocket and dabbed at her brow. "Horses can be such frightening animals. Especially those brutish brumbies. If I had my way they'd all be sent off to the abattoirs. They're nothing but a nuisance to station owners."

"The stallion doesn't remind you of Blazer?" Roslyn asked curiously.

"Blazer?" Kim's straight brows drew together in a frown. "You surely don't mean Sir Charles's old hunter?"

"Yes."

"Oh, don't be absurd!" Kim said in her brittle voice. "And you're supposed to have a good eye."

"Not only supposed to. *Have*! Marsh thinks the same. Here he comes now looking like Chief Thundercloud."

In fact Marsh was striding towards them, his whole aura radiating a dazzling authority. He had pitched his

hat away in a fit of aggravation and one coal-black wave
fell onto his dark copper forehead adding to the impression of rugged vitality.

His blue eyes were like lightning as he stared at them,
then without a word, he seized Roslyn, pulled her into
his arms, and held her in a fierce, biting grip.

"Lord Rosa!" He sounded as though he was under
intense pressure. "If I hadn't got a rope to that
stallion..."

"You *did*." She stood on tiptoe, getting her mouth to
his chin. Her body curved into his, drawing and giving
superlative comfort.

Neither of them took account of Kim who stood aghast
at the sight of them locked so tightly together. She sucked
in her breath, sharply agonised, then blurted, "Don't
worry about *me*, Marsh. Worry about her. She's perfectly all right." The muscles of Kim's throat were so
tight her voice was almost hoarse. "It was splendid the
way you lassoed that murderous brumby."

Marsh threw up his head, looking back at her. "The
brumby was doing what all wild horses do. It was taking
a desperate chance," he observed harshly. "I can't say
much for the way *you* acted. You simply looked after
yourself. In the process putting Roslyn in worse danger.
The two of you could have taken shelter behind the Jeep,
instead you sent her crashing to her knees."

Kim's haughty, high-boned face flushed a mottled red.
The colour even stained her throat. "It was an accident,
Marsh. It wasn't intentional."

"It was a fearful *mistake!*"

Kim looked at him imploringly, just managing not to
cry. "I *told* Roslyn I was sorry."

"Yes, she did, Marsh. Kim didn't have time to think.
She had to move." Roslyn had received poor treatment

at Kim's hands for years but she found she had no desire to retaliate.

"You're right, Roslyn. You're right." Kim looked at the younger girl with a kind of desperate gratitude. "It was just one of those terrible moments in life."

"The split-second decision that can make or break," Marsh said grimly.

"I do regret it." Kim wrung her hands, her habitual arrogance quite crumpled away.

Looking at her Roslyn decided. "We can and will forget it," she said, applying a little pressure to Marsh's arms in an effort to get him to lighten up. "Friends, Kim, okay?" She held out her hand.

"Yes, indeed!" Kim moved quickly to shake Roslyn's hand. "It's very kind of you to see things my way."

Roslyn's smile was touched with a little irony. "I have my points."

"I might go back to the homestead now." Kim looked back towards the Jeep. "I feel a bit shaky."

"Pour yourself a brandy. A large one," Marsh suggested, sounding less daunting. "I'll have one of the men drive you back. I'll have to stay here and supervise."

"They didn't have the top rails high enough." Kim sought to divert attention from her.

"They would have been only the stallion's no ordinary brumby. He has quite a look of Dad's Blazer."

"I noticed it," Kim answered, more in her ordinary tone. "At least I noticed it after Roslyn pointed it out. Will you come back with me, Ros? There's no need for you to stay here."

"She's staying." Marsh spoke emphatically. "I don't want her out of my sight until my nerves settle." He looked over to the holding yard, where Lucky was perched on the top rail. "Lucky," Marsh called. "Get over here, mate."

"We ought to do something for him," Roslyn ventured.

"I intend to."

"What have you got in mind?"

"Enough to induce him to give up brumby running. He's had one too many crashes for my liking."

"He's brave!" Roslyn watched Lucky limp toward them, his face split in a grin.

"Isn't he!" Marsh's tone left little doubt of his opinion of those who weren't. "Now it's his turn to be rewarded."

"But it's not necessary," Kim said.

"Why don't we walk over to the Jeep while Marsh speaks to Lucky," Roslyn suggested.

Lucky was blushing in anticipation of a grateful slap on the back. Roslyn knew it would never enter his head he was about to be assured of a windfall.

"That was good of you to take my part the way you did," Kim murmured, almost painfully as they waited beside the Jeep. "Marsh seems to be disgusted with me. I've never, ever, disappointed him before."

"Don't dwell on it, Kim."

"I expect I will." Kim glanced away. "Do you suppose he'll tell the girls? A recount of the incident could make my part in it look worse than it really was. I was in a genuine, breathless panic. We all know horses but they can be scary creatures."

Roslyn wasn't prepared to let her off quite so lightly. "Kim, only for Marsh, Lucky and I would have been right in the line of fire."

"Dammit, I know that too well. I can't decide whether the bike rider was brave or he'd taken leave of his senses.

It's not as though he was getting anywhere with that busted leg.''

"The great thing is, he *tried*.''

"Yes." Kim gave a mirthless smile. "All's well that ends well, so they say. I hope the girls are as understanding as you are. They'd hate me forever if anything had happened to Marsh.''

"Perish a thought for Lucky and me! Why don't you say one of the brumbies made a break for it and Marsh lassoed it in. They'll accept that. They're used to Marsh and his extraordinary feats.''

"Of course, that's it!" Kim ran a hand over her sun-streaked hair, looking down in distaste as her palm came away smeared with red dust. "Lord, I'll have to take a shower and wash my hair. You look a sight, as well. Marsh is a genuine hero all right, but he can be so very intimidating at times, don't you think?''

"No question about it!" Roslyn smiled, realising this was probably the first time Kim had been on the rough side of Marsh's cutting tongue. Well, serve her right!

It was evident at dinner Kim had given her own version of the afternoon's events to Justine and Dianne, but neither Roslyn nor Marsh sought to contradict her.

"The perfect whitewash!" Marsh commented later as he and Roslyn were waiting on the veranda for Justine to join them on their after-dinner walk. "I'm only surprised she didn't make herself out the heroine of the piece.''

"Maybe that was due to your rather sardonic expression. Kim's not comfortable being in the wrong.''

"She doesn't hesitate to come down strongly on everyone else. Must give her a sense of power. Before

Ju-Ju turns up, how about a grateful kiss? It's already hours overdue.''

"Sure, a pleasure!" She intended to keep it light but his arm encircled her, drawing her into the shadow of a vine-wreathed white column.

"Marsh, someone might come."

His blue eyes gleamed. "Am I supposed to care? Your place is in my arms and that's where you're going to stay."

"We'll tell them very soon," she promised.

"Why not the hell *now*?"

"Not with Kim here. Not a chance. I don't want to see her pain."

"For a little fire-eater, you're surprisingly tender-hearted." He bent his head and began to trail his lips down her cheek. "Your skin is so smooth...so cool. It's like satin. It has a lustre. I'm waiting for when I can kiss every inch of it!" He turned his attention to her mouth, kissed it roughly, sweetly, until she clung.

"Wild thing!" he muttered, feeling the fever in her.

"You're my hero!"

"I *know*. Also, when you can get your act together, your *husband*."

"What kind of husband are you going to make?"

"Don't expect bashful."

She felt an incredible spring of joy. "Not bashful, *no*!" Ardent, urgent, warm and tender, a flawless, imaginative lover who could make her body dissolve with desire. Just standing within the circle of his arms, having his beautiful, sensuous mouth touch her skin, was dizzying. It created an immense *need*.

"I'm only human, Rosa," he murmured. "I'm even considering sleep walking."

"I'm sorry. I'm stuck with my vow."

"And I'm stuck with *you*."

"Were you ever in love with Kim?"

"What do you think?" he asked crisply, lifting his head.

"Curious, nothing more."

"I don't blab," he said in a dry, laconic voice.

"I don't, either, but I am involved."

"So long as you know that." He grasped a handful of her hair. "If I must tell the truth, *you're* my only passion."

"Yet you found the time to fit in a few others?"

"Rosa, I had to do something to keep myself from going mad."

"Men are the devil!" she said in a soft, helpless undertone, her need for him so desperate it threatened to override all else.

"And I intend to take advantage of it." He touched a hand to her breast, then pulled her into his arms, pressing his marvellous mouth down on her own.

Waves of flame.

Scorching her... searing her.

This was Marsh and he had the power to destroy her.

CHAPTER EIGHT

MIDMORNING of the following day when even the gum leaves were turned edge on to the sun Roslyn went back to the homestead in search of a cold drink only to walk head-on into a confrontation with Kim. She was barely inside the house, her riding boots beating a tattoo on the patterned tiled floor when Kim came flying down the central staircase, her face wearing a furious expression.

"So there you are!" she cried, advancing on Roslyn who stood rooted to the spot in sick dismay. Did it *ever* stop? "It was just too much to expect, wasn't it? That's what comes of a lack of breeding. You can't be trusted to act with honour. Well, you can stop playing your games around me, you devious little bitch!"

Close up Roslyn could feel the heat coming off Kim's tall body. Her own face darkened but she fought hard to hold on to her composure. "What compels you to attack me?" she asked. "What gives you the right? You talk of *breeding*. You're no one to admire."

"And you *had* to tell the girls?"

"What?"

"Oh, don't act the innocent. Don't make me sick!" Kim cried hotly. "How *could* you when you promised? You've humiliated me dreadfully. Perhaps lost me my dearest friends."

"Kim, you'll have to explain yourself," Roslyn said in a quiet voice that lost nothing in intensity. "Otherwise I'm going in search of a cold drink."

138

"You'll damned well stand still and listen to me!" Kim reached out and grasped Roslyn's arm, her long fingers digging into the skin.

Roslyn shook her head. "Take your hand off me, Kim. I don't respond to this kind of approach."

"Oh, I hate you. I hate you," Kim said. "Why did you ever have to come back? We thought we were shot of you forever!" She threw off Roslyn's arm and immediately Roslyn stepped back.

"But I'm here, Kim and I'm staying," Roslyn said with quiet dignity.

"Then bear in mind you're not *wanted*."

"Marsh is the only one I'm worried about."

"Of course!" Kim gave a discordant laugh. "But when are you going to get it into your head he'll never take you seriously? He doesn't respect you. He doesn't—" She broke off as tyres crunched on the driveway and a moment later Marsh started up the steps, halting on the threshold as he sensed the anger and tension that bound the two women.

"Anything wrong?" he asked briskly, his burning blue eyes moving from Roslyn to Kim.

"No." Roslyn was reluctant to go into it, but Kim laughed incredulously.

"No, she says, when her underhand actions have bitterly hurt and humiliated me."

Marsh's expression went grim. "Hey now!" he protested, moving further into the entrance hall.

Roslyn put out a hand to him, seeking to avert a worse scene. "Kim is upset about something. I don't know what."

"Then she'd better explain herself. What's your problem, Kim? Maybe we can straighten it out?"

Kim turned to him in an attitude of appeal. "You can't trust her, Marsh, as you'll soon discover. You're playing with fire encouraging this girl. She's not one of us."

"It might be a good idea, Kim, if you minded your own business," Marsh responded in such a cutting voice Kim's face crumpled.

"To say that to *me!*" she cried, unable to conceal her hurt. "After all we've been to each other."

"Kim, we haven't been anything to each other for years," he contradicted her flatly.

"You *loved* me!"

He spread his hands. "I'm sorry, no. You knew what we had the brief time we spent together."

"It was wonderful!" Kim stared at him, her heart in her eyes. "I'll remember it always. Always!"

"That would be downright foolish," Marsh responded, still with that tough slant.

Roslyn found she couldn't bear it. She had never been much good watching someone else's pain. "Please excuse me," she said. "My throat is quite parched."

"Hah!" Kim suddenly cried, blocking Roslyn's way. "It's this girl, isn't it? This little nobody whose mother is in your employ."

Marsh's blue eyes flashed sparks. "Your snobbery is appalling. And it beats me why!"

"What about your sisters, then?" Kim challenged. "Do you know how they feel?"

Marsh shrugged. "I had hoped they'd drop into the twenty-first century. It's long overdue. But so far as Rosa's concerned, my sisters have no say at all. If Rosa and I want to get married, we will."

Kim's imperious, high-boned face blanched. "Married? Whoever mentioned the word? Not even Roslyn would be such a fool."

"I mentioned the word," Marsh told her grimly. "Rosa's been holding out on you but I don't mind telling you I've asked her to marry me and she's agreed."

Kim stood like a woman faced with the ungraspable. "You're joking," she said finally. "It's just a cruel joke. You want to get back at me."

"That's a big job! Actually, Kim, on this occasion I didn't give you a thought."

"Ah, *no*!" Kim wasn't yet persuaded, locked into her own vision.

"What made you tell her, Marsh?" Roslyn asked, distressed.

"Don't be ridiculous, Rosa!" he said with crisp impatience. "It needed saying. I've gone along with your idea long enough. It hasn't come off."

"I don't believe this!" Kim stared from one to the other though her gaze seemed unfocused.

"I'm sure you do," Marsh responded.

"Not marriage, *no*! Your mother detested this girl. And her mother. She'll be here to haunt you."

"Oh, my!" Marsh said with a derisive smile.

"I must go home!" Kim cried, realising her plans had been shot to pieces.

"Whatever you think best." Marsh shrugged.

"Take a little time to calm down, Kim, please," Roslyn begged, but Kim turned on her with loathing.

"How can you speak to me like that after all you've done? You couldn't wait to reduce me in Dianne's and Justine's eyes."

"How is that?" Marsh asked curtly, infinitely more aggressive than Roslyn.

"I'll tell you how," Kim said in a harsh voice. "She told them about that incident yesterday when she promised she wouldn't. She made me out a coward in the girls' eyes."

"No!" Roslyn brushed her dark glossy hair off her face. "You're quite mistaken."

Marsh's tall, lithe body went tense. "A liar she is *not*! If Rosa said she didn't say anything, she didn't. Why don't we get to the bottom of the matter right now?"

"Why not?" Kim agreed harshly, breathing fast. "At least you'll find out what your precious *Rosa* is really like."

Marsh's expression turned daunting, but he didn't reply. He turned away, leading them through the house until they found Dianne and Justine deep in conversation on the rear courtyard overlooking the pool.

Both young women broke off in their conversation as the others approached.

"Hi!" Marsh said in such a clipped tone Justine rose to her feet.

"What's up?"

"A little matter to be cleared up." Marsh swooped on the big, fringed umbrella, adjusting it so Dianne was completely in the shade.

"Thanks, Marsh," she said, looking up. "You seem upset?"

"You've got it in one! Kim seems to think she's been shamed by something Roslyn said to you both regarding the incident with the brumby?"

"Oo-oh, need we talk about it?" Dianne nearly wailed. "So unlike Kim. I can scarcely believe it!"

"What makes you think Ros told us, Kim?" Justine demanded.

"Well, didn't she?" The words exploded out of Kim with furious impatience.

"Not at all!" Justine spoke very coldly and distinctly. "Marsh and Ros allowed us to believe your version. It was Mrs. Earnshaw who put us in the picture. She considered your action put Ros into considerble danger. Let alone Marsh! She wasn't about to kowtow to your desire to protect yourself."

"Well, thank you, Justine!" Kim sounded cut to the heart.

"Mumma told you?" Roslyn asked Justine in amazement.

"That's right!" Justine turned to her. "She was very angry about it. She didn't think she was under any obligation to cover for Kim. As far as that goes, Kim's overdue for a setdown. She's been barely civil to Ros and her mother for as long as I can remember. I suppose if Mrs. Earnshaw ever comes back to Macumba as Lady Mortimer, Kim will fall down before her."

"That'll be the day!" Kim gave a hard, ironic laugh. "Harry's probably not serious at all. Once he gets back to his own people he'll forget all about her."

"It just kills me you've done this, Kim," Dianne said sorrowfully. "The consequences could have been dreadful."

"I thought you *wanted* Roslyn out of the way?" Kim gripped a chair and shook it.

Dianne's mouth fell open. "Come off it, Kim! I've always had a problem with Ros. No question about it. I think it started when I kept growing and growing and Ros stayed petite."

"Good God!" Kim said in disgust. "So you'll settle for having her as a sister-in-law, will you?"

Dianne straightened abruptly. "A *what*?" she demanded with some vehemence.

"I would have liked to tell you myself," Marsh interjected, "but Kim is bent on vengeance. Afterwards she's promised to pack up and be on her way. Rosa was giving you time to settle but it seems to be out in the open now. I've asked her to marry me and she's agreed."

"But you *can't* marry her!" Dianne gasped, and fell back among the cushions. I'll go insane with Roslyn for a sister-in-law."

"Oh, shut up, Di," Justine said briskly. "You know you're talking rubbish." She turned to Marsh and Roslyn, who had drawn closer together. "I'm offering you both my love and very best wishes right now. I truly believe you'll be very happy together."

"Thank you, Justine." Roslyn inclined her head as Justine bent to kiss her.

"What a turncoat you are!" Kim cried scathingly. "I'm shocked. *Shocked*. Just you wait until the word gets around."

"Concerning *what*?" Marsh asked with such asperity Kim sobered abruptly. "I'm not a good man to cross."

"None of us are!" Dianne said sharply. "So don't go spreading any gossip around."

"It could be you're all mad!" Kim cried emotionally. "I'm not among friends anymore. I'll go pack."

Less than twenty minutes later Kim had herself organised to leave.

"You're all going to regret this!" she cried out in the hallway. "There's no way Marsh can marry that girl and have a happy life."

Despite protests she didn't want them, they weren't friends, Dianne and Justine accompanied her to the airstrip, Justine at the wheel of the Jeep. "Very bad manners not to have," Dianne declared afterwards. "I'd like you to know, Ros, I warned Kim against spreading any malice. If you *must* be part of the family, we'll all have to pull together."

"That's very kind of you, Di," Roslyn answered politely, trying hard to look suitably grateful.

Olivia wasn't in the least perturbed she had precipitated the crisis. "There's no such thing as keeping something like that quiet on a station," she told Roslyn when Roslyn approached her about it. "Even when she gave her version I somehow didn't believe her. Young Jessie told me in the kitchen this morning. She got it from her dad. He was *there*. I can tell you no one was impressed with the high-and-mighty Miss Petersen. I know you and Marsh were prepared to let it pass, but I saw it more as a strike for us. I've nursed quite a bit of resentment about Kim Petersen's treatment of you."

"I felt sorry for her all the same." Roslyn sighed. "She was mortified in front of the girls and she's still in love with Marsh."

"It's called tunnel vision. I've been guilty of it myself," Olivia murmured wryly.

"So what's the latest on Harry?" Roslyn asked.

Olivia brought tea to the table and poured it. "It appears his cousin has rallied a little but the doctor thinks it was only to keep himself going until Harry arrived. It's quite marvellous the will to hang on. Harry wants me to come over for a bit after Christmas. Out of the question with a big wedding to be arranged."

"Of course it's not, Mumma. It's just what you need and it will settle things for you and Harry. Have you made any decision?"

Olivia shook her head. "You know me, darling. I'm a real ditherer. It's such a *big* decision. I'm very fond of Harry. He's a good friend. We're so comfortable together, but this baronetcy has thrown me a bit. I've known enough snooty people to last me a lifetime."

"There are lots of nice people, too, Mumma. The *real* people. Besides, there's no need to give everyone a rundown on your life. Let them judge you on how you look and act. I know Harry will be proud of you."

Olivia gave a worried smile. "Have you considered, darling, his feelings might have undergone a change?"

"A great big no to that!" Roslyn answered firmly. "Harry has a constant heart. He wants you over. My advice is to make a booking."

"I have a stepbrother and two stepsisters, you know," Olivia said, and tears suddenly welled in her eyes. "I used to love them when they were little."

"Look them up. It's entirely possible they'll welcome you with open arms."

"Not if they've turned out like Delia." Olivia sighed. "How have the girls been since Marsh sprang his bombshell?"

"Okay," Roslyn said. "'We all have to pull together' was the way Di put it." Roslyn gave an excellent imitation of Dianne's haughty tones.

"Well, Justine is nowhere near as stuffy as she used to be," Olivia commented. "Marriage has improved her no end. Dianne has a way to go. By the way, the Shepards are arriving tomorrow afternoon. You couldn't ask for better references. They'll take up their duties immediately but I'll be on hand to help out. We'll have lots of visitors between now and Christmas."

"Marsh told me he fully intends to introduce me as his fiancée," Roslyn said in slightly troubled tones.

"Good." Olivia gave her daughter's hand a sharp pat. "I never thought he'd go along with all that business of keeping quiet. It's not his style."

"No. But then Marsh has never been in my position. Anyway, the girls took it a lot better than I thought."

"I don't know whether to applaud or to cry. You could take your place anywhere. And you'll have to remember Kim Petersen is bound to try to cause trouble."

"Then she runs the risk of alienating this family," Roslyn retorted sharply, suddenly realizing it was true.

The very next day the first of the visitors descended from the sky to be followed by dozens more. Once Roslyn counted thirty light aircraft scattered like birds off the strip. The girls' husbands arrived in the middle of this migration, bearing stacks of gifts. It was obvious they had been informed Marsh and Roslyn were to marry but Roslyn privately considered both of them had difficulty taking it in. Only one name had loomed on their horizon. Kim Petersen. It had generally been agreed she was the most impressive candidate.

How things had changed!

As for the stream of visitors they professed to a man to be delighted Marsh had at long last decided to take a bride. The news had spread like wildfire from station to station courtesy of Kim Petersen, so all of them had had plenty of time to absorb the shock. What did fascinate them was the revelation "good old Harry" was now Lord Mortimer. All gave Olivia their best wishes to pass on, apparently unsurprised Harry and Olivia were considering making a match of it.

Meanwhile Mr. and Mrs. Shepard went about their business with a social stiffness and a pompousness that jarred Roslyn in particular. They were extremely competent as their references had stated, but Roslyn would have liked more natural behaviour and less formality. She tried to indicate this, she hoped diplomatically, but

it soon became apparent the Shepards intended to stick
to their inflexible code. The family didn't seem to notice.
They had long been used to having servants around them
and, generally speaking, treated them as though they
weren't there. It didn't suit Roslyn at all. Obviously
courteous behaviour was essential but the stiffness put
her off.

"So change them later on," Olivia advised. "As mistress of Macumba you'll be able to do as you like."

"Mistress of Macumba!" Roslyn cried softly. "Lady
Faulkner will turn in her grave."

"Does that scare you?"

"No." Roslyn shook her head. "What really bothers
me is the way Chris still likes to hang around me. What
an ass! It's no wonder Di gets jealous and resentful. I've
tried insulting him but nothing seems to put him off.
Not the fact he's married, or this ring." She held up her
left hand adorned with a diamond ring of exquisite
design.

"The marriage is solid enough," Olivia considered.
"It's just that you fascinate him. My own view is he's
well on the way to getting a punch in the nose. Marsh
is fed up with him. He's fairly well fed up with Justine's
husband, as well. All those long boring accounts of his
professional brilliance. Maybe the Shepards could go to
him. I think they'd suit."

One way and another the festive break turned out to
be a stressful time, which somehow got worse as the days
rolled on.

"I don't think our holiday is turning out a success,"
Justine told Roslyn privately as they took a late afternoon
ride together. "I never realised how boring we all are.
Not you, of course, and heaven knows, not Marsh, but
the rest of us. Ian is only thirty-five yet he's starting to

sound like an elder statesman. He really is a dear, you know, but taking silk had such an effect on him. I was going along with it, but now I can see he takes himself much too seriously. One can see those Rumpole stories aren't all that exaggerated. And, of course, Chris, if he continues, will set off a calamity. I saw Marsh's face last night. I wondered how he checked himself."

Roslyn sighed. "I don't give Chris the slightest encouragement. Rather the reverse."

"Oh, we know that!" Justine exclaimed in disgust. "It's not a serious thing. Of that I haven't got the slightest doubt. It's more a silly moth around a flame sort of thing. You *are* so much more beautiful than the rest of us. It can be very unsettling. I think we'll get away earlier than intended. See the New Year in, then fly off home. One thing I've been meaning to say to you—" Justine turned a prim face to her "—with your mother joining Harry in England you *can't* stay here with Marsh. There will be quite enough chatter as it is. I want you to come to *us* until the wedding. You'll need help getting it all arranged. It could be such fun! Organisation is my job. It's where I come into my own."

"I hadn't thought about it, Justine," Roslyn said when she had given the matter a lot of consideration. "I still have my own house."

"And I'm sure it's very pretty, but let's face it, ours is better. We're undertaking this as a family. Everything must be done *right*. Marsh told me you're giving a big gala party for everyone we can't fit into the wedding. I can help you with that. I know everyone you will need to get to know. I thought possibly the big reception room at the Beaumont. They do things extremely well and it's so central. Black tie, of course. I'll be your matron of honour. Di will be too far gone to act as an attendant.

Don't you worry about Di." Justine paused reassuringly. "Once she gets used to the idea she'll be as excited as I am. You'll have to help us with our outfits. You're so good with that sort of thing."

And so it went on for almost an hour.

"I don't want you going anywhere," Marsh said when Roslyn attempted to discuss it with him. "Not even for a day."

They had managed to find a moment alone together, taking the four-wheel drive to the edge of the sandhill country. The mirage was abroad, creating fascinating visual effects. In the distance shimmered a long billabong where there was no water to be had, with curious, sticklike figures dancing delicately above the silver glitter.

"I suppose we have to be seen do the right thing," Roslyn reasoned. "There will be enough talk without our being alone together at the homestead."

"How could we possibly be alone with the Shepards in attendance?" Marsh asked with extreme sarcasm.

"I thought you were happy enough with them?"

"Listen, I'd have been better off hiring a couple of actors. They're much too stiff and formal. But I can't see us getting replacements until the New Year. I'll just have to pay them off and mark it down as a mistake. The agency handled it. Next time you'll have to do it."

"They'll be *different*."

"That's all right with me. Macumba is a homestead, not a stately home. Another one I might just consider chucking out is Chris. His behaviour is only tolerated in adolescence. Obviously you've lost nothing of your old witchery."

"I've tried to be as offputting as possible," Roslyn said mildly.

"A little difficult when you haven't got the knack."

"I could try growing a beard," Roslyn joked. "You sound disgruntled."

"Clever you! Actually I'm as mad as hell. If I didn't have Di to consider I'd bundle him onto the first plane home."

"It's not serious, Marsh. Justine put her finger on it. It's a sort of harmless crush."

"It's not harmless and it's not amusing," Marsh answered with a little rasp. "Di must be finding it very embarrassing."

"She hasn't mentioned it to me."

Marsh shrugged. "Knowing Di, there's no guarantee she's not saving it up. I never thought I'd say this, but I'll be glad when they all go home."

"Justine thought just after New Year."

"She's a darling!" Marsh said feelingly. "I don't go along with her idea of taking you, though."

"Mumma has offered to stay as chaperone, but I said no. No one is trying to rush her into marrying Harry, but the fact of the matter is, she does need a little push."

"Come on, a big push," Marsh drawled.

"You are out of sorts!" Roslyn allowed her eyes to linger on his face.

"*I want you.*"

"I want you, too." Her voice was husky. There was colour in her creamy skin. She was about a second away from admitting *how* much.

"So what's the stand-off?" he asked edgily.

"You might abandon me after you have your wicked way."

"Don't start that again, Rosa," he warned in a dangerous voice.

"All right. Let's say I don't want to land us in a crisis situation."

"Crisis? *What* crisis? God, we're engaged."

"I have the ring." She spread her small, elegant hand, manoeuvring the diamond ring, a central two-carat stone flanked by baguettes, into a beam of sunlight. The glitter was dazzling. "Four carats in all, isn't it?"

"Closer to five."

"It's unbelievably beautiful."

"Nothing beside you." Instead of loverlike it came out as a soft growl.

"You just want to get me into your bed."

"As soon as possible," he assured her crisply. "What do you think is going to happen to you? You'll fall pregnant?"

"Would you want that?"

He looked at her, his eyes drowningly blue. "I surely would," he said in a heart-stopping voice. "I'd even shed a few tears. But I want you to *myself* for a while."

After you abandoned me for years? It sprang into her mind automatically, evidence even now as his promised bride she couldn't overcome the raw pain of the past. Damaged people took a long time to heal, she thought, but managed quite coolly, "That sounds very loverlike, but I, for one, don't want to anticipate our wedding night."

He touched a hand to her cheek, pretended to shiver as if a chill lay on her skin. "Are you sure you won't want to order up a couch for me in the dressing room?"

"No. I'll stick to my side of the bargain."

He was silent for a little while, staring out at the savage beauty of the sweeping plain. A hawk that had been hovering overhead suddenly made a leisurely swoop on a group of zebra finches feeding on the ground. The little birds made no attempt to get away. They never did.

"You're enjoying this, aren't you?" he said.

There was something like a taunt in his vibrant voice. "Why would you say that?" she parried.

"Because I *know* you, Rosa." He held her chin. Made her look at him directly. "I know your fears and your resentments. I know what shapes you. Drives you. You were powerless once. You're not going to allow it to happen again."

"That's only sensible, isn't it?" The old hostility was alive around them.

"Being sensible isn't the motivation," he said, and released her. "It's more like punishment and we both know why." He switched on the ignition, turned to her. "Go back with Justine if you think you should. I won't try to stop you."

CHAPTER NINE

IT TURNED out to be a hectic time. Roslyn had been staying with Justine and her husband, Ian, in their beautiful harbourside home for just on three weeks and already she had lost count of the number of social gatherings she had attended. Justine was determined on introducing her to all the people she thought Roslyn should know. Legions it seemed. She badly missed Macumba. Most of all she missed Marsh. She had spoken to him on the telephone several times since she'd arrived but they were strangely stilted conversations that left her feeling isolated and vulnerable. Their gala party was scheduled for the coming Saturday night. Marsh had promised he would be in Sydney by Friday afternoon at the latest, piloting his own plane. He would be staying with Justine and Ian, as well, taking advantage of the large, heritage-listed house Ian had inherited from his maternal grandmother.

As the house and grounds were so large it had been decided instead of the Beaumont as originally planned the party would be held at the house. Something that pleased Roslyn and Justine took in her stride. They hadn't seen a lot of Dianne who didn't appear to want to be a part of all the endless social rounds, the planning and preparations for the party and the wedding. Her pregnancy was an excuse in part, but Roslyn had to accept she and Dianne would never really get on. A fact of life and one she could live with. Justine, on the other hand, had been a tower of strength. As she'd claimed, organization was her forte and she was thriving on all the excitement and bustle.

"Planning makes perfect!" she told Roslyn constantly, her countdown guide, her blueprint for success, never far from her hand. "Everything is going to be splendid, you'll see. Weddings have a way of catching everyone up."

The invitations would go out the following week, a month before the ceremony would take place on Macumba. All the attendants had been chosen, Roslyn had asked two of her closest friends from her university days to be bridesmaids. Justine would be matron of honour. Not for a moment had Roslyn considered anyone else. Gowns for the bridal party had been settled on and were in the process of being made by a top designer who specialized in exquisitely romantic bridal wear. The same designer had been given the task of making Roslyn's gown for Saturday night but as she was losing weight a small adjustment to the waist and bodice had to be made.

She spent an hour at Bridal House standing tirelessly while her party gown then her wedding dress were refitted. The designer had a wonderful stock of gowns, fabrics and accessories but nothing more beautiful in Roslyn's opinion than her own wedding gown which was nearing completion. It was a midsummer's dream in lace and silk: the long, line-fitted lace bodice, off-the-shoulder and long-sleeved, tapered to a central peak, the wonderful silk skirt billowing from the hip. Bodice and a deep hemline of the skirt featured the same exquisite pearl beading. Her headdress was a very beautiful and delicate circlet of handmade flowers in pinks, palest yellow and magnolia with little sprays of pearls to simulate baby's breath. It was a very romantic look and

Roslyn thought it was perfect for her. So did the designer and her clever team who were counting on a lot of publicity.

Justine, who never figured herself the "romantic type" would wear the very flattering fitted sheath with a small hat and a spotted eye veil Roslyn had suggested. It all worked and everyone was delighted with their outfits. Roslyn should have been in a state of euphoria, instead she was conscious of high emotion fraught with pressing anxieties. Justine was being marvellous, indeed they had grown surprisingly close, but Roslyn wanted her mother home. They talked frequently but it wasn't enough. Olivia had given Harry the answer he most wanted in the world. They were to be married in London soon after the "super wedding" as Harry had dubbed it. That meant Roslyn and Marsh could attend. Olivia was due home in a few days. Plenty of time for the wedding but Harry, deep in family business, would remain in England for as long as possible. It was Harry who was to give Roslyn away. Harry, the perfect gentleman. Harry, the English lord. Justine considered this an enormous asset.

When Roslyn arrived back at the house shortly before noon she was told by Justine's housekeeper that Mrs. Herbert and a friend were in the Garden Room where lunch would be served. Justine had a wide circle of friends. Roslyn wondered briefly if she'd already met her. The same people seemed to turn up at every large gathering. She went directly to her room to tidy up then found her way back downstairs to the Garden Room so called by the family because it was filled with lush green plants and marvellous hanging ferns, furnished informally and looked out over the beautiful grounds and the sparkling blue harbour beyond.

Roslyn was almost at the door, arranging her face into a pleasant smile when she heard Justine's friend speak.

"Well, with all *your* help, darling, it should be a wonderful occasion. Roslyn doesn't know just how lucky she is."

Roslyn felt the sudden intense heat of anger. Kim Petersen. She had to have a hide like a rhinoceros! The thought of her still stalked Roslyn. The spite and the rage Kim had displayed. But why should she feel so shocked? It was inevitable they would see Kim Petersen again. The Faulkners and the Petersens had been lifelong friends. Elaine Petersen and Lady Faulkner had been close confidantes, fellow schemers. It was understandable Kim's aberrant behaviour might be forgiven.

Roslyn took a deep breath and entered the room, unaware her golden eyes were *burning* in her face.

"Ah, there you are, Ros!" Justine called from her chair, not exactly looking like she had been enjoying her chat. "You'll never guess who's come to call on us." The tone was slightly dry.

"It couldn't be Kim?"

"Hi, there Ros!" Kim put her blond head around the back of her peacock chair, her voice bright and friendly, her eyes as hard as agates. "I'm in Sydney on a shopping spree so I thought I'd call in and say hello."

Roslyn hid her disgust perfectly. "How are you, Kim?" she asked calmly, taking a chair facing the entrancing view.

"Splendid!" Kim smiled, showing her fine white teeth. "You've lost weight, haven't you? You look tired."

"All the excitement!" Roslyn ignored the little flash of malice.

Justine nodded. "Justine's been telling me all about it. It's quite an achievement to take Sydney by the storm."

"Have I done that?"

"Justine appears to think so. Look, what I really wanted to ask you both, *beg* really, was not to hold my little outburst at Christmas against me. I deeply regret it. I assure you such a thing will never happen again."

"That's good to hear. It was an unpleasant experience," Roslyn said, looking straight at her.

"And I've said I'm sorry." Kim tried her best to look humble but only succeeded in looking dogged. "Justine and I have been friends all our lives. I can't imagine life without her and Di. If you'll allow me, Ros, I'd like to be friends with you."

Roslyn stood up, walked to the French doors, then turned back. "Is that possible, Kim?" she asked in a quiet, reasonable tone.

"Oh, please, do sit down again," Kim implored. "I think so. I hope so. It will be very difficult if we're not. The family is expecting an invitation to the wedding."

Justine, looking perturbed, made a sweep on her countdown guide.

"Is this a joke of some kind?" Roslyn asked.

"I didn't imagine, Kim, you would want to come." Justine stirred restlessly in her chair.

"Of course I want to come!" Kim cried. "There would be too much talk if I wasn't invited. Besides, Mum and Dad were your parents' close friends. It's clear we *have* to be invited."

Roslyn sank back into her chair. "It's not clear to me. It's *my* wedding after all. It's generally understood I invite the people I like."

Kim seized the legs of her linen slacks and pulled them down over her knees. "All right, I know you have a perfect right to say that, given my behaviour, but you must realise I'm no longer any threat."

"I wouldn't write you off all the same," Roslyn said dryly.

"Surely it would be too painful," Justine asked in a near puritanical voice.

"You overestimate my feelings, Ju-Ju," Kim's grey-green eyes blazed up. "I know I've wasted a great deal of my life hankering after Marsh. That's all over. He's made his choice. He wants Ros. Actually life's picked up for me. Craig and I are thinking of getting engaged."

The relief on Justine's face was enormous. "You *are*? But that's marvellous. Craig's always been in love with you. I couldn't be more delighted. Have you told Di?"

"As a matter of fact I have. I rang her as soon as I arrived. She sounded quite out of sorts, poor darling. Craig is in town right now as a matter of fact. He has business to attend to. Actually his fondest wish would be to meet up with Marsh. Neither of us is doing anything Saturday night. Would it be too much to ask an invitation to the party? If Craig's thinking of a best man he wouldn't go past Marsh. You don't mind, do you, Ros?"

"That's a tough one. I think I do."

"It would mean so much to me. To us both." Kim fished in her Gucci bag, pulled out a handkerchief and actually touched it to her eyes. "You've no idea how our little falling out has weighed on me."

"Please, Kim, don't upset yourself," Justine said, looking distressed.

"I've been punished enough. I knew I had to come to you both and beg your forgiveness. Di's so sweet. She told me she could never turn her back on me."

"That's all right, I wouldn't either," Roslyn said in a wry voice. "You and Craig are welcome to come along Saturday if it's so important to you. Does that suit you, Justine?"

"That would be just fine," Justine murmured, her expression indicating the opposite.

"Lovely. *Lovely*! I'll get myself something extra special to wear." Kim jumped up, insisting on kissing them both. "Marsh due in Friday?" she asked as she resumed her chair.

"How did you know?" Roslyn heard her own voice sharp with challenge.

"Di told me," Kim answered sweetly. "Justine told me your wedding dress is almost finished, Ros. What's it like?"

So you can spread it around as the latest intelligence? Oh, no!

"That's a secret," Justine said before Roslyn could even speak.

"Why not!" Kim gave a merry laugh. "You'll make a beautiful bride, Ros. Ju-Ju's been telling me you've been better than a sister helping her make herself over."

"She's created my new image!" Justine declared with touching gratitude. "I've never bothered much with clothes, as you know, but there's no doubting they make the person. I have an entirely new wardrobe. Ros decided on my hairstyle and my new makeup, as well."

"I swear I couldn't believe my eyes!" Kim declared jarringly.

Justine did, in fact, look striking in just the way her mother's looks had commanded attention. Her thick, wavy hair, her great asset, was beautifully cut and groomed, her skin polished, cared for and deftly made up. Roslyn had steered Justine away from her conservative wardrobe to one with a more dynamic character. It revolutionized Justine's "look" showing to advantage her lean lines and tawny lioness colouring.

"Where did you get that silk shirt?" Kim suddenly demanded, staring hard at the distinctive cinnamon shirt.

"*I* picked it up," Roslyn answered, realizing Justine was momentarily stuck for words. "But I can't remember where." If she'd said where she'd bought it the chances were Kim would be right up there.

"You're staying to lunch, Kim?" Justine asked faintly.

"I'd love to!" Kim nodded her head with enthusiasm. "Something good on the menu?"

"Cheeseburgers," Roslyn said wickedly.

Midmorning Friday the grounds were invaded by workmen who erected three huge, pure white marquees around the garden and pool area. The same firm took care of the linen, crystal, cutlery, china, chandeliers, chairs and the fairy lights for the trees. In the afternoon a floral decorator would arrive to fill the house and the marquees with flowers, various swags and all the indoor plants they would need including tubs of standard ficus. The food would be handled by another service, providing what was confidently expected to be a sumptuous buffet and a bar service. One group of musicians would play under their own canopy in the garden. Another had been hired to play in the old ballroom in the house. In all one hundred guests had been asked, but sadly, in Roslyn's opinion, that number had been upped by two. The weather held perfect.

Roslyn was enjoying a short rest in her bedroom that afternoon when she heard a car sweep up the driveway and come to a stop at the foot of the steps, its engine ticking over. It had to be Marsh. He'd told them he would take a taxi from the light aircraft terminal. She rushed to the window and looked out, her heart racing so fast she actually held a hand to it. It *was* Marsh! She emerged through the front door as he stood out on the driveway paying off the driver. He looked wonderful from all angles. She loved the back of his head, the set of his shoulders, the way their width tapered to his lean, taut waist, terrific butt and long legs. She felt such a flood of love she flew down the steps, hair and pleated skirt whipping in the bay breeze.

Keep what we've got at all costs, she thought. One day he'll tell me he loves me.

Marsh turned, flashed his wonderful smile, threw out an arm.

How to describe his reaction? *Rapture*. She moved into the charmed embrace, feeling his arm close strongly, urgently, around her. Her loneliness lifted miraculously. She turned up a radiant face and he seemed to glide into kissing her; no affectionate greeting but a kiss that left her feverish and clinging.

"So how is my promised bride?" he asked, his blue and brilliant eyes intent on her expression. "Surely you've lost a little weight?"

"All the partying," she explained. "I've lost count of the luncheons and dinner parties. How was your flight?"

"Too slow. I couldn't wait to see my beautiful Rosa."

"I've missed you." Her voice shook a little.

He looked at her for a long moment, touched her hair that in the sun had the sheen of a dark plum. "If that isn't the darnedest thing! I think you mean it." There was a faint twist to his beautifully shaped sensuous mouth.

"Don't you believe me?"

"Convince me when we're on our own."

"In fact I can't wait."

He laughed under his breath. "So, absence does indeed make the heart grow fonder."

"You haven't said you missed me."

"You mean that kiss didn't get through to you?" He lifted his dark head, saw his sister waving as she came through the front door and out onto the veranda. "Say, Ju-Ju looks great!" he exclaimed with some satisfaction.

"Doesn't she!" Roslyn stood away happily as brother and sister exchanged bear hugs.

"You've been hiding your light under a bush," Marsh said after a low whistle.

Justine flushed with pleasure. "Ros can take the credit. She's nothing less than a magician."

Marsh moved back. Seized Roslyn around the waist. "Haven't I always said there was magic about her? You look very stylish, Ju-Ju. Keep it up."

"Ian's thrilled," Justine confided. "He keeps telling me I look compelling."

"And he's not wrong!" Marsh put an arm around both women's waists. "Plenty of activity going on?"

"You're going to pay for it, darling," Justine said gleefully. "No expense spared for Marsh Faulkner and his divinely beautiful fiancée."

Roslyn laughed a little ruefully. "What exactly *is* the connection? people ask, then rush into the next question before I can tell them. I suppose they'll wake up one day."

"No need for any secrets," Marsh said firmly.

"You can tell everyone Lord Mortimer will be giving you away," Justine said slyly. "A lot of people are still impressed by a title."

"Not *me*," Marsh said crisply. "It's what people *are* that counts."

"As I'm learning," Justine said, leading the way into the house. "I suppose you'd better know Kim Petersen is back in our lives."

Silence for a moment. "Why not?" Marsh said in a jaded tone. "There's something unstoppable about Kim."

"I fear so." Justine moved into the living room and they followed her. "She turned up the other day. Said she was on a shopping spree. Wanted us all to be friends."

"Dear Lord!" Marsh made a derisive sound. "More like she wanted invitations to the wedding."

"How did you guess?" Roslyn gazed up at him.

"*Darling*, it's going to be a big, social event. It may even turn out to be the biggest event of the decade if what's going on here is anything to go by." His glance swept the glorious flower arrangements and the festive appearance of the room. "Kim will certainly want to be there. Her mother, too, even if her nose will be very slightly out of joint. They'd be devastated to be left out."

Justine nodded. "I guess so."

"Well, she won't be the *bride*," Roslyn observed brightly.

Marsh took her hand, carried it to his mouth. "That's *your* role, Rosa. You're the only one who can fill it."

"How gorgeously romantic!" Justine cried, and clasped her hands. "Getting back to Kim—"

"*Must* we?" Marsh groaned. "She can't dictate our lives."

"Here, here!" Roslyn agreed heartily.

"I was only going to say she told us she's getting engaged to poor old Craig, which is a great relief."

"Well, the poor devil has lived in hope. The relief, I doubt. Personally I'll believe it when it happens." Marsh drew Roslyn down onto the sofa beside him. "Black coffee and maybe a sandwich, Ju-Ju, if that's no bother. I haven't eaten since first light."

"*Really?*" Roslyn looked at him with the utmost concern.

"No Shepards to pack a picnic lunch," he said dryly.

"We'll soon fix that!" Justine made immediately for the door. This was her beloved brother. There was nothing she wouldn't do for him. Except tell him Kim had virtually invited herself and Craig to the party the following night. Roslyn would have to do that. She was so happy for them. Surely Kim couldn't come along to spoil it.

At seven o'clock on the night of the party Roslyn stood before her long mirror surveying the effect of her beautiful gown. It had been ruinously expensive but well worth it. She had never looked better, but then, she had never owned such a gown nor indeed been invited to the sort of function where she could wear it.

In keeping with the designer's romantic vision, the dress was almost a ballgown in the grand tradition. Scarlett O'Hara might have worn it! Roslyn couldn't describe the colour of the sumptuous silk taffeta. Fern green, willow green, green shot with gold? It was very unusual, but so soft and seductive. It made her eyes glow strangely. Her "witching" look as Marsh put it. She touched a hand to the full, short sleeves, puffing them still further. The neckline—what was it, portrait?—

framed her shoulders, the décolletage a little lower than she'd wanted but the designer wouldn't have it any other way. It was a bravura gown. A tantalising glimpse of bosom was de rigueur.

Because of the *Gone With the Wind* overtones Roslyn had decided to wear her hair in a loose, dark cloud at the back, but drawn up at the sides. She had some very pretty pendant earrings she intended to wear. Her face was a little pale. Perhaps a touch of blusher? She had to admit she was nervous. This was the first time she and Marsh would appear together before all his friends. It struck her now as extremely odd she had given in to Kim Petersen's emotional blackmail and allowed her to come. It had been nothing less than that. For all Kim's avowals of friendship and the news of her pending engagement, which Marsh had taken with a large grain of salt, Roslyn feared there had been something almost sinister in the depths of Kim's eyes.

A little shiver ran through her and she turned away, comforted by the lovely, rich swish of her billowing skirt. What to wear around her neck? She had an Art Nouveau necklace that might do. It didn't match the earrings but she had often worn them together. In fact they'd been much admired. She *did* have good taste. Justine's transformation had been extraordinary. It gave her a great deal of satisfaction. As did their bonding. Of course Justine would do anything for her brother but there was no denying a genuine friendship had sprung up between them. Justine was a kinder, more sensitive person than her sister and light-years away from the late Lady Faulkner. A veil of sadness, of old memories, settled on Roslyn that she tried to shake off. She must take hold of her new life. Recognise her own value. A few people, it was true, had greeted her with speculative eyes. But for the most part she had been welcomed with warmth by all the people Justine had insisted she meet. The fact that she could play the piano extremely well had been a help. When Dame Agatha returned from her overseas lecture tour she would find the right moment to thank her for all she had done. It was a great pity she'd had to grow so many prickles to survive.

A knock at the door interrupted her thought. She went to it expecting Justine, but finding Marsh in evening dress on the threshold. He looked so splendid surely her eyes were exposing her heart?

"Rosa, darling, you're a living dream! Here, stand back. I want to take a look at you."

"You won't believe the bill!" She stretched out her two arms and stepped into a waltz, looking over her shoulder and smiling at him as she dipped and swayed. The bright brilliant light shone on her, struck a dazzling light in her eyes. She felt faintly unreal. Perhaps it was all a dream?

"The awful thing is I can't do what I want," Marsh said in a deep, thrilling tone.

"Which is?" She broke off gracefully to stand before him.

"Kiss you and kiss you and kiss you. Never stop."

"That would be wonderful," she whispered.

"Don't close your eyes or I'll forget everything," Marsh said in a soft warning. "Will we *ever* get a moment together?"

"That's my prayer. That's my dream."

They stood staring into one another's eyes until finally Marsh remembered what he'd come for. "You'll want something to wear around your neck. This should do admirably." He handed her a long, narrow box covered in midnight-blue velvet.

"Jewellery?" Her own eyes shone like gems.

"An expression of my undying love."

"I don't know if I can stand this."

"I think you can. Open it."

Roslyn did so, at the same time giving a soft, little gasp. "Marsh, how exquisite!"

"Not very, beside you. Shall we try it on?"

"*Please!*" She lifted her hair away from her neck and turned. "I've never had such a gift."

"Don't think it's your last." He secured the catch, his fingers warm and tingly at her nape. "Let's take a look." He took her hand, drew her to the long mirror and stood just behind her, his hands on the tips of her shoulders. "I don't think you know how beautiful you are."

Roslyn stood staring at her reflection in some awe. The necklace lay against the creamy skin of her breast; lustrous pearls linked in gold, a diamond centrepiece from which was appended a diamond set opal heart. Brilliant flashes lit the deep glowing black gem. Blues, greens, fiery reds, the topaz of her eyes.

"You've had it specially designed." She brought up a hand to trace the outline of the opal heart.

"Of course, with you in mind. I know you love opals. The heart is symbolic."

"I'll treasure it all my life."

"As I'll treasure the vision of you." He bent his head, his lips finding the little depression above her collarbone. "My beautiful Rosa!"

Sensation was so exquisite, so melting, she let her head fall back as his hands came up gently, but so sensuously beneath her breasts. She put her own hands over his, guiding them higher. Her body craved his so badly the stress was enormous. Her breasts throbbed with pain.

His voice murmured endearments into her ear, soft, intimate, infinitely seductive.

I'm dying with love for you, she thought. Marsh, my destiny!

"Oh, this is impossible," he said. "I can't kiss you. Spoil your makeup. So help me I just could go crazy."

"Love is often described as a madness, didn't you know?" She dropped her hands, giving a shaky little laugh.

"Tell me you love me, Rosa," he said. "We're alone." His expression was taut and brushed with a faint violence.

"Marsh...you can't know...I..."

Whatever she was going to say he was not then to know. The bedroom door was ajar and after the briefest of raps Justine came bustling through. "Darlings!" she cried. "We'll have to take up our positions downstairs to receive our guests." Her eyes fell on Roslyn's necklace and she checked abruptly. "Nice," she said. "Very nice. Glorious but not vulgar. A rare thing, like you, Roslyn. Now look here, you two! I'm not going to burst into tears. It took me a solid hour to put on my make-up." She touched her forehead, gave it a little worried rub. "Earrings, what about earrings?"

"What's the matter with me!" Marsh exclaimed. "They're here in my pocket."

"Of course they are. I knew they were," Justine said. "You never forget anything." She swooped on Roslyn suddenly to kiss her satiny cheek. "All right? Not nervy?"

"Not now." Roslyn clipped the earrings, large pearls surrounded by a twist of gold, to her ears.

"Fan the sides of your hair out a bit," Justine advised, a striking figure in a white, one-shouldered, toga-like garment. "Now, come downstairs, darlings. Ian wants us to pose for a few home photographs. Don't expect them to be professional, but he *will* keep at it!"

By nine o'clock the party was in full swing. People roamed the grounds and the main reception rooms to a heady flow of music, laughter and streams of conversation. The buffet tables, covered in starched white damask sagged a little under the wealth of dishes; honey-glazed hams, stuffed roast turkeys, differently prepared chickens. There were silver platters of just about every kind of seafood served on beds of ice; whole smoked salmon, lobsters, prawns, oysters, scallops, crabs and oven-baked mussels. Quails eggs were piled up in bowls and there were salads of all kinds. Hot dishes were served, as well; Thai and Indonesian, splendid in their presentation and accompanied by traditional rice. A separate table had been set up for sweets from delectable, mouth-watering light mousses to the richest, wickedest chocolate gateaus and tortes. Waiters in black trousers and short, natty jackets circled continually with champagne, classic cocktails, Kir, Bellini's, Buck's Fizz and nonalcoholic drinks.

At different times the level of noise almost drowned out the band on the lawn but they continued to play their hearts out to an ever-changing, appreciative audience.

The quality of dressing was superb. The black tie of the male guests complimented the beautiful dresses their wives and girlfriends had chosen. Lots of expensive jewellery had come out of bank vaults for the occasion. There was even one tiara Roslyn thought a bit idiotic until she was presented to a genuine European princess of fabled glamour. She shook Roslyn's hand, smiled at her and said, "So lovely. So very lovely!" The v's were pronounced as deep f's. Roslyn realised she was being honoured.

By ten-thirty she thought she would need at least a week to recover. She drank only mineral water or orange juice so she could keep her mind together. No way was she going to become the slightest bit intoxicated.

Apart from the fact she didn't want to, she knew her every gesture, her every move was under scrutiny. Yet she felt happy, confident, unfazed by all the introductions. Most people seemed delighted to meet her. Not critical at all. Some *did* eye her off speculatively. Older women mostly. Probably friends of the Petersens. But in the main she felt she was making a good impression. Marsh's blue eyes every time they rested on her, conveyed enormous pride and pleasure. How could she *not* shine? Even Dianne smiled happily and waved, every time they passed her. Dianne had taken to growing her hair out. With her pregnancy well established she had gained a soft bloom. Chris must have been threatened with all kinds of things because his manner, though friendly, held none of the usual silly flirtatiousness. Perhaps the thought of fatherhood was maturing him.

Kim and Craig had arrived late. Kim standing a statuesque three inches over Craig's head. She was dressed to kill in bright red chiffon. The dress hung on shoestring straps and the skirt was slit in several places to show her spectacular legs. The colour brought out her golden tan and the gilt streaks in her blond hair. Roslyn thought she looked stunning, but her gaze was a little odd. A surprising mix of supreme self-confidence with a decided dash of defiance. Beside her, Craig faded into nothingness. He was prematurely losing his hair, which was sad, but he had inherited a quarter share of the family business with an estimated personal fortune of around 55 million dollars. He was known to be paranoid about publicity but with Kim on his arm he was beaming broadly.

"For Pete's sake, couldn't you have told me?" Marsh demanded as he and Roslyn moved forward to greet them.

"I tried, but I just couldn't find it in my heart. That doesn't mean I'm not going to keep an eye on you."

"Oh, don't be absurd!" Marsh laughed. "I only hope they're going to spring a surprise and announce their engagement. It'd be just like Kim to break the good news at *our* party."

"It *is* possible," Roslyn said.

Instead Kim took Marsh by the arms, leaned forward and kissed him full on the mouth. "Darling, my congratulations! This is a wonderful occasion."

"Indeed, indeed!" Craig added hastily, giving Roslyn an uncertain smile. "It was sweet of you both to invite me when you heard I was in town. You look absolutely beautiful, Roslyn. A knock-out!"

"I want to steal your necklace," Kim smiled. "Marsh's present, am I right?"

"Of course!" Roslyn put her hand on Marsh's arm and he hugged her to him so her billowing skirt swayed. "An expression of our love."

"Opals are a bit too unlucky for me," Kim said with a tiny shudder of unease.

"Surely you're not superstitious?" Craig asked, looking embarrassed. "I think it's the loveliest necklace I've seen and it suits Roslyn perfectly."

Kim patted him and rolled her eyes. A kind of what-would-*you*-know? "The house looks splendid, all the decorations and everything. Did Di make it?"

"But of course!" Marsh said, sounding surprised. "Di would never miss an occasion like this."

"Mmm," Kim looked as though she had heard differently.

"Ah, there are the Munros," Marsh said, his gaze going over Kim's head. "Would you both excuse us? I'll catch up, Craig, later on. A few things have happened you might like to know about."

Kim looked momentarily devastated as though some of it could be about her, but it would be business, polo, something like that.

"Watch Kim tonight," Marsh warned Roslyn as they moved off. "She has a decidedly malicious streak. More, with a few drinks in, she's nutty enough to do anything."

"So why did I say she could come?" Roslyn answered in a wry voice.

"I'm sure we'll live to regret it. She gives me the impression she's out to make trouble."

After supper Roslyn retired briefly upstairs to repair her lipstick. She looked fine and that soothed her. So far the party was progressing amazingly well. Kim and Craig had merged in with their friends. Was it possible Craig could control her excesses? He *was* a hard-nosed businessman after all.

Roslyn decided to take the rear staircase to the ground floor. She would be much less on view. As she commenced the descent to the first landing she realised a group of women was having a conversation in the shadowy privacy of beneath the stairs. She hesitated a moment, unsure whether she should keep going or retrace her steps and take the main staircase. For no reason she could understand she had a sinking suspicion Kim might be one of the women. Marsh was right. Kim had a kind of aura tonight. It conveyed a certain "I'm going to have my little revenge." Not exactly smart. Roslyn herself wouldn't care to confront Marsh head-on. Nor Justine and Ian if they considered themselves insulted. But Kim would gossip *in private*.

Before she could take another step Roslyn had her proof. *Kim*.

"Oh, I know she looks good, but she's desperately unsure of herself."

Another woman snapped back, "You'd have fooled me! I thought her incredibly poised. I wouldn't have taken her for a modest little schoolteacher at all. Carol was telling me she plays the piano awfully well. I adore the classical piano. I'd love to hear her play."

"You wouldn't enjoy it as much as you think," Kim came back. "Her style is very over-the-top."

"Darling, would *you* know? You don't know anything about music," another voice said. One Roslyn knew. Anne Fletcher. "It beats me why you wanted to come tonight. We're sorry Marsh has been snatched from you. We know you're very upset, but it's all history now. He's made his choice. Accept it."

"I'd dearly love to but I'm finding it a little hard after all we meant to each other. This marriage would never happen if Lady Faulkner were alive."

"Not that awful woman!" Anne Fletcher moaned with black humour. "Did you ever meet with such coldness and arrogance? The time she gave the girls, yet she was ruthlessly possessive of Marsh. Not that he tolerated it for long."

"Very tragic Sir Charles was killed," another voice said. "Snatched away in the prime of life. Such a pity the marriage wasn't a success."

"You can blame that on the little bride's mother. The housekeeper," Kim said with such vindictiveness it made

Roslyn ill. She wasn't going to listen to this. She put her hand to her long skirt, lifted it, but again Anne Fletcher broke in, staying Roslyn's intervention.

"I'm sure we'd all prefer if you didn't mention that, Kim. You're being incredibly bitchy tonight. You and Marsh were never *that* close. Besides, I don't believe that old gossip for a minute."

"Then you *should*!" Kim maintained in a steely voice. "Mother and daughter, both opportunists. Roslyn latched onto Marsh and wouldn't let go. The mother got her hooks into Harry Wallace when all else failed. He's Lord Mortimer now by the way. I suppose you've heard. It's quite bizarre! The Faulkner housekeeper will most certainly become Lady Mortimer."

"Good for her!" yet another voice said. "Why should the rich have all fun!"

"You're not terribly supportive!" Kim complained, obviously stung by the group's reaction.

"Not very," Anne Fletcher agreed. "We've all been friends with the Faulkners since forever. We're not about to fall out now and for *what*? I can't see that they won't be divinely happy together. Now, I'm for a drink. Anyone else coming? Doesn't Justine look marvellous tonight? She's finally got herself together."

The women moved off and Roslyn proceeded down the stairs. She felt upset by what Kim had said, particularly about her mother, yet heartened by the lack of response. Anne Fletcher was a leader in young society and obviously ready to embrace Marsh Faulkner's wife. Kim would have her nose well and truly out of joint.

Sometime later Marsh told her many of their guests had expressed the wish to hear her play the piano. "You don't mind, do you?" He looked at her, his eyes brilliant. "I thought it would be nice if you did."

"I don't mind in the least."

"I'm sure they'd be very appreciative."

"Besides, Ian is already lifting the lid."

Marsh lowered his head suddenly and kissed her cheek. "Show them what you're capable of. You have quite a repertoire. What about the 'Ritual Fire Dance' to start seeing we're all on a roll, then maybe one of the Chopin études? I like the one that goes all up and down the piano."

"The 'Ocean Étude.'" She smiled. "It's a very good thing I haven't touched a drop of alcohol. Bravura performances just don't happen unless one's in total control."

Marsh laughed gently and led her across a sea of smiling, expectant faces. Roslyn arranged herself at the piano, pushed the long piano stool back a little, cleared her long full skirt from the pedals and her feet. Finally she was comfortable and announced in a calm voice her two choices. The "Ritual Fire Dance" by Manuel De Falla and Chopin's famous étude in C minor. Clapping broke in a wave over the large drawing room. All the French doors were open to the veranda so the music would float out over the lawn. Someone had obviously told the band to stop so the level of noise had dropped dramatically. Many of the guests had heard Roslyn was a gifted pianist but only a handful had actually witnessed a performance.

Near the double doors leading to the hallway, Kim hissed in Craig's ear, "For God's sake, how boring! Anyone would think she was a famous concert pianist, when she's strictly an amateur. I'm going for some fresh air. You stay if you want."

"I'd like to," Craig said, sounding shocked. "It might be a good idea, Kimmy, if we toddle off shortly after. You've had one Bellini too many."

Vulnerable to criticism at the best of times, a heated flush rose to Kim's cheeks and she looked back wild-eyed. "Don't tell *me* how to conduct myself, Craig McDonald, you little squirt!"

"Squirt?" Craig savoured that for a moment. "How very delightful!" He turned away deliberately.

Kim waited for no more. She stalked unsteadily into the packed hallway and made for the front door while the thrilling opening bars of the "Ritual Fire Dance" spilled out into the night....

Roslyn sat with Marsh, wonderfully relaxed and happy. Her little recital had been a brainwave. It appeared to have established her in her own right. Marsh was telling a story that had everyone laughing when a waiter came to stand at her shoulder.

"I'm sorry, Miss Earnshaw," he apologised, "but Mrs. Herbert would like to see you for a moment in the Garden Room."

Roslyn left immediately, signalling to Marsh with a little wave of her fingers. Probably it had something to do with the handful of guests who weren't behaving as they should. What Roslyn could do about it she didn't know. Justine mightn't like the idea but she could be forced into suggesting they might like to go home.

When she reached the Garden Room, which wasn't open to their guests, she found it very dimly lit. The great hanging ferns and the golden canes in glazed pots stood out in sharp silhouette against the backlit glass wall which was a blaze of dull gold. Across the hedge of sasanqua camellias she could just see couples walking and beyond that people dancing on the lawn.

"Justine?" she called, just starting to think something was amiss. Justine wouldn't be standing about in the semi-dark.

"Roslyn?" a voice cried back from somewhere in the shadows.

She felt a flash of rising irritation. "Is that you, Chris?" She walked towards the sound. "What are *you* doing here?" Surely to God it couldn't be a replay of his and Dianne's engagement party when he'd cornered her for a kiss. "A bit of fun" as he'd put it then. "Chris?" she repeated sharply.

"Keep your hair on. Here I am." He was suddenly there, pressing her arm. "Justine sent a message she wanted me. I expect she has a problem with the sillies in the pool."

"Who told you?" Roslyn demanded.

"I'm sorry?" Chris responded in his supercilious tone.

"Who told you Justine wanted you?"

He touched her hair. "Oh, a waiter. I'm sure it was a waiter."

"Well, she's not here. It might be a good idea to find the light switch."

"Just when I was enjoying it in the dark. *I* don't know where it is. You've been living here for weeks."

Roslyn moved back to the door. "I have, but I don't think I've turned the lights on here once. One would expect to find the panel somewhere here, but it's not. Frankly I think we should leave."

"What, when you've done your best to get me here!" He laughed.

"That'll be the day!"

"I wonder. I'd say you planned all this."

"For what purpose?" she asked coldly.

"Trouble-making, I should think. That would suit you. You *are* a troublemaker as we all know. That business at Christmas was your doing. How gauche to imply I was bothering you."

With her eyes adjusted to the gloom Roslyn saw his expression plainly. It disgusted her. "Are you quite mad?" she demanded. "I never said a thing."

"I'm sorry, Ros, I don't believe that. Marsh was just about ready to throw me out. Di was livid. Upsetting her at such a time. I love her. We've never had such unpleasantness."

"That's a downright lie. You'll always have unpleasantness while you can't seem to stop yourself from chatting girls up."

He stared at her in outrage. "Chatting girls up? I assure you I'm only being pleasant. Most girls love it."

"Well here's one who doesn't! It's my opinion someone has set *us* up. It's not me and even you couldn't be so dim-witted."

"Dim-witted? Oh, hell, yes. That's why I'm so successful. I do believe your little triumph has gone to your head. If there's any mischief going on, probably you have something to do with it. Of course I know what it is. You're put out I haven't paid any attention to you all evening. Kim's right. You muscled in on this family. You've tried to make a fool out of me."

Roslyn saw red. "From where I'm standing, I wouldn't *have* to try!"

He gave a derisive snort. "You don't fool me, Ros. You and your sharp little tongue. Not that it isn't part of your charm. I suspect you're a vixen at heart. I want you to know if you cause any more unpleasantness—"

"You'll do what?"

"I won't have Di upset," Chris said in a pious tone. "You've been causing these upsets for years. I want it to stop."

"Give me strength!" Roslyn exclaimed. "*You* want it to stop when I'm the one who's had to put up with your stupidity. You make me sick!" By now, Roslyn, in a fine temper went to turn on her heel, but Chris caught her arm, the expression on his face equally angry, but excited, too.

"Oh, really? Well, *I* think you've always been attracted to me."

"Let go of my arm, Chris," Roslyn snapped.

"We've got a few things to clear up first."

"Then let's clear them up in front of Marsh and Dianne."

"So you've got Marsh in the palm of your hand." Chris jeered unpleasantly. "It's only a temporary thing. He'll start back up with Kim. They understand one another."

"I said *let go*!"

"Shut up. Shut up for a minute," Chris urged. "There's someone coming this way."

In another minute one of the doors leading to the terrace opened and the room was flooded with light.

"Hey, you guys!" a teen-aged, bedraggled apparition cried. "Are we breakin' up a little tryst?"

Chris dropped Roslyn's arm in horror. "What in the world are you doing here, Marcy, and in that condition?" To make it worse, the girl was accompanied by Kim Petersen, who looked at Roslyn and Chris with open disgust in her eyes.

"Just can't leave it alone, can you, Ros!" she said with contempt.

Marcy giggled, obviously intoxicated. "Naughty, naughty, Chris!"

"Don't be ridiculous!" he said, looking devastated.

"It don't look good," Marcy crowed. "Though why in the world anyone would look at you when they had Marsh."

"I think you'd better stop right there, Marcy," Roslyn warned, suddenly producing her most quelling schoolteacher tone, "or repeat what you're saying in front of my fiancée, Dianne and your parents."

It had some effect because Marcy appeared to sober abruptly. "Hang on, hang on. I was only trying to take the heat off me."

"Then I assure you you haven't succeeded. I take great exception to your implication."

"So I apologise. Absolutely," Marcy replied, peering earnestly through her long, sopping hair. "Hey, wait a couple of ticks. Kim insulted you, as well. Make *her* apologise. Make her apologise, too, for giving me a glass of champagne and daring me to jump in the pool."

"I did nothing of the kind!" Kim protested vigorously, giving Marcy a push in the back.

"You did so, too!" Marcy accused her. "Ask Craig. He fished me out. I've been drinking orange juice all night. Then one drink and it hit me like a bomb."

"You're dripping water all over the floor," Roslyn said dispassionately. "We're of a size. I can lend you something to put on, then maybe we should think about getting you home."

"I've never done anything like this before," Marcy suddenly wailed. "Mum'll kill me."

Just as another wail went up Justine, who had been informed of the incident, appeared. "Gracious, Marcy, what a really foolish thing to do!" Oblivious of her expensive dress she went to the girl and put her arm around her. "You've always been so sensible, too."

"I only had *one* drink, Justine," Marcy said almost indignantly. "Kim gave it to me, but she won't admit it."

"Because it's not *true*!" Kim said coldly. "The first thing you should learn, Marcy, is to admit your own mistakes."

"Where's the bathroom," said Marcy. "I feel sick."

Justine led her away hurriedly and Roslyn decided to speak her mind.

"I knew when you arrived tonight, Kim, you'd planned some little incident to discredit me or spoil the party."

Kim looked unimpressed. "My dear, you have the problem of explaining to Dianne what you were doing here in the *dark* with her husband."

"She sent me a message," Chris said, on Kim's side.

"You're pathetic, Chris!" Roslyn exclaimed. "You don't have to explain anything to Kim. She set the whole thing up. I suppose she popped a little extra into that girl's drink. She's unscrupulous enough. The Garden Room has been off limits to our guests. Why bring her in here? The pool house would have been a better idea. It's well stocked with towels and robes."

"I wanted dry clothes," Kim declared in her superior voice. "I knew perfectly well Justine wouldn't mind. I know the house well."

"You certainly know where the light switches are. I overheard you talking to your friends earlier in the evening, the unkind things you said about me and my mother."

"Well, you know what they say, darling." Kim sneered. "Eavesdroppers et cetera."

"You didn't get much for yourself, either."

"So what's going on?" a voice demanded. They all looked around as Dianne made her way towards them, her forehead creased in a frown. "There's a party out there, doesn't anyone know? Ros, Marsh is looking for you everywhere. Anyone would think you've been kidnapped!"

"I'll go to him," Roslyn said, anxious to avoid any further embarrassment.

"She's going to run, just like she did the last time," Kim said to Dianne in a harsh, ugly voice.

"What are you talking about, Kim?" Marsh, who had combed the house, finally found them in the Garden Room. He spoke forcefully, his handsome face stirred to anger.

"She's going to ruin everything for you," Kim cried. "Do you think I'd be speaking out only the old ties run deep? Roslyn is the catalyst amongst us. She forces change."

"The complications of love!" Dianne cried. "I wish I knew what you're on about now, Kim. This whole business has affected you."

"Then let me explain." Kim's eyes flashed around, her face flushed with drink and recklessness. "It's the old story. Conquest. She's done it before at your engagement party. Some weird trait in her character—"

"As I recall, you were the one to bring it to Mother's attention," Dianne interrupted as though she had suddenly thought of something significant.

"I *had* to. Then as now. Roslyn is the sort of woman who won't let go. She needs all this admiration. She's missed out on so much. She doesn't care you and Chris are happily married. You're pregnant. She arranged to meet Chris here. Alone."

"Incredible!" Marsh made a sound of utter disbelief. "Is that the best you can do? And I imagine you've been working on it for weeks. Rosa stole away to meet *Chris*? You'd better lay off the booze."

"It's the way it happened," Kim said in a furious voice. "I have a witness. Marcy Hallett. We surprised them."

To Roslyn's utter horror Dianne began to weep. "Di, *please*, this is nonsense. Chris and I haven't the slightest thing to feel guilty about. We were both told Justine wanted to see us here. She didn't. It was a pathetic scheme Kim thought up. I'd say she even brought along something to lace my drink, only I wasn't having any. *Anything* to discredit me."

"Chris believes me," Kim said. "Perhaps he knows Roslyn better than any of us."

"You rattlesnake!" Roslyn went white.

It was the last straw for Marsh. "You might like to leave, Kim," he said in a hard-edged voice. "There's no way I'm going to allow you to ruin *our* night. I'd like to make it perfectly plain I believe that was your intention."

His words and the way he said them filled Roslyn with all the confidence she needed. *Our night*. Their shared happiness. The certainty she was very special. Everything about him spoke of love and commitment!

Yet Kim persisted, locked in to the delusions she had long nourished. "Hate me. Go on, hate me. It can't be helped. I'm your friend, Marsh. Di and Justine have been like my own sisters. There's a lot of feeling in our relationship. I'm vitally interested in the Faulkner good name. Roslyn Earnshaw is a wild card. I admit she looks and acts the part, but she's a *fake*!"

"Fakes get exposed. Rosa is the real thing."

"She's taken every opportunity to drive a wedge between the family." Two hectic spots of colour burned in Kim's face. "I loved you, Marsh. So badly. We were going to spend our lives together. You *promised* me, you know you did. After we made love we used to lie so gently, so quietly, making plans for the future."

"You don't want to sell your story to the newspapers, do you?" Marsh asked in a caustic voice. "They print pure fiction.'"

Kim put a hand to her heart, a gesture that could have been poignant only for the touch of theatre. "I know, too, I'm *not* lying!"

"Ah, God, Kim," Dianne said, and her voice broke. "Why don't you just shut up? There's always been a dark side to you."

"Forgive me, pet." Kim reached over and touched Dianne's tawny hair. "It's as bad a thing as I've ever done upsetting you."

"Excuse me before I throw up," Roslyn said abruptly, turning to leave.

"Not on your life!" Marsh caught her around the waist, holding her to him. "This is *our* party. The others can leave."

Kim threw up her head, lifting her body to its full height. "I'm sorrier than I can say it's turned out like this, Marsh. I only thought to warn you as a lifelong friend."

"*Out!*" Marsh said in no uncertain tone.

"You love me, darling, don't you?" Chris asked as he led his wife away.

"I don't know. I honestly don't know."

"It hurts me to see you so upset, Di," Kim cried, hurrying after them.

"I can imagine!" Dianne's voice floated back, the tone as dry as ashes.

"My poor, sweet Rosa," Marsh groaned, dropping a kiss on the top of Roslyn's head. "But don't say I didn't warn you."

"It's just obscene the things she says."

"Blame it on her childhood," Marsh said laconically.

"And you. It all goes back to you."

Marsh smiled, his mouth curving ironically. "Not a fight, Rosa. Not now. I couldn't stand it. It's been a perfect evening. You've been wonderful. I'm so proud of you."

His blue eyes were as clear as a rock pool. She could see her own reflection. "That means *everything* to me, Marsh. Your total trust and commitment. You haven't even heard the full story."

"Darling, if it's all the same to you, I really don't want to know," Marsh said with dry humour. "I'd like to drive Kim into the desert and leave her there. She's supposed to be Di's friend yet she couldn't care less about upsetting her."

"I'd say from Di's tone that's truly sunk in. Chris might have a time calming her. It's really terrible the tickets he has on himself."

Marsh looked at her, tipped her chin, smiled. "Hey, it's *our* party remember?"

"I love you," she said, the last barrier down, her most secret thought uttered.

"Say that again!" His blue eyes glittered with such an extraordinary light she felt irradiated.

"I said, I love you. I love you. I love you. Forever and ever!"

His arms closed around her, a little rough, a little fierce. "You've taken your time."

"I was wounded, Marsh."

"Tell me you're healed?"

She stared up at his beloved face; a face of passion and power. "As long as you allow me to become part of you."

His arms tightened urgently. "But, Rosa, you've always been that. You *must* know. You're the flame in my heart. The love of my life. That's all there is to it, what we've always known in our souls. We love each other."

"Why has it been so difficult to *say* it?"

"We lost a little trust in each other for a time. We let too much of the past stand in our way, but that's all over. You're going to bloom as my wife, Rosa. I want to love and cherish you and give you all the things you've been denied. I want you to become my partner in all things. I want you to use and display your gifts. I want our children. Our mutual creations. You're the only woman in my life, my adored Rosa."

"You used to be a *fantastic* lover!" she whispered.

"*Used* to be?" he said, laughing. "I'd better tell you—"

"Kiss me," she begged with loving intensity. "I need you to—"

"Lord, Rosa!" he muttered, his handsome face taut with high emotion. He kissed her then, elated by the response he met. She was beautiful...beautiful...her mouth a flower that opened for him. He had dreamed of the day she would tell him she loved him again. He couldn't fully express his love. Not tonight. Nor the next. Part of the manifestation of their love was something spiritual. In just under a month they would be married on Macumba. Their wedding night would be one they would remember forever...

"Marsh!" Roslyn gasped, almost overcome by the blaze that had sprung up between them.

"Just showing you how it's going to be." He placed his hands on the sides of her face, his thumbs tracing the lovely line of her jaw. "Remember our secret place?" he murmured.

Irresistibly Roslyn's mind turned back. "How lonely I've been for it. A billion desert stars, the white limbs of the ghost gums glowing in the purple night, the scent of the boronia and the lovely little mauve mist that grew in great numbers around the lagoon, the crunch of the sand beneath us, the wind song at intervals whistling through the trees. I used to dream of it endlessly. Our magic place. Our magic time. We belonged then. But we were torn apart."

"We've reclaimed our dream, Rosa," Marsh said with great depth of feeling. "Just as we can reclaim our supremely beautiful secret place. We can go back on our wedding night. It would be easy to slip away."

She was quiet for a moment, afraid she might cry. "That would be *perfect*!"

"So, it's a date?"

"It's a promise!" Her golden eyes filled with a radiant light.

Marsh bent his dark head, claiming her mouth in a kiss that began slowly then surged into desire.

All this Justine saw as she bustled into the room having dealt with young Marcy, who was still feeling the effects of her earlier dip, and Kim and Craig who had made a swift exit on the verge of a few words. Justine had nearly wept with relief. She was an absolute dolt allowing Kim to come.

"Darlings, darlings!" she cried, and got through to them on the fourth try. "Plenty of time for all that. Decades and decades! Everyone wants to know where you are.''

"Just a quiet moment together, Ju-Ju," Marsh said languorously, lifting his handsome head.

"And tremendously touching it was, too!" She smiled indulgently. "But we must return to our guests. Marsh, would you mind having a word with the band? They don't seem to be paying any attention to Ian. The volume is enough to loosen your fillings. Ros, you might like to touch up your lipstick. Marsh seems to have kissed it off. Honestly, I haven't felt so good in years. Tonight has been wonderful but you've no idea how much I'm looking forward to the wedding."

Marsh's blue eyes met Roslyn's over his sister's tawny head. "Never as much as we are," he said.

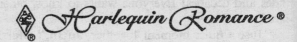

New from Harlequin Romance
a very special six-book series by

DEBBIE MACOMBER

The town of Hard Luck, Alaska, needs women!

The O'Halloran brothers, who run a bush-plane service called **Midnight Sons**, are heading a campaign to attract women to Hard Luck. *(Location: north of the Arctic Circle. Population: 150—mostly men!)*

"Debbie Macomber's *Midnight Sons* series is a delightful romantic saga. And each book is a powerful, engaging story in its own right. Unforgettable!"

—Linda Lael Miller

TITLE IN THE MIDNIGHT SONS SERIES:

UNLOCK THE DOOR TO GREAT ROMANCE AT BRIDE'S BAY RESORT

Join Harlequin's new across-the-lines series, set in an exclusive hotel on an island off the coast of South Carolina.

Seven of your favorite authors will bring you exciting stories about fascinating heroes and heroines discovering love at Bride's Bay Resort.

Look for these fabulous stories coming to a store near you beginning in January 1996.

Harlequin American Romance #613 in January
Matchmaking Baby by Cathy Gillen Thacker

Harlequin Presents #1794 in February
Indiscretions by Robyn Donald

Harlequin Intrigue #362 in March
Love and Lies by Dawn Stewardson

Harlequin Romance #3404 in April
Make Believe Engagement by Day Leclaire

Harlequin Temptation #583 in May
Stranger in the Night by Roseanne Williams

Harlequin Superromance #695 in June
Married to a Stranger by Connie Bennett

Harlequin Historicals #324 in July
Dulcie's Gift by Ruth Langan

Visit Bride's Bay Resort each month wherever
Harlequin books are sold.

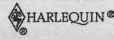

HARLEQUIN PRESENTS®

Harlequin brings you the best books, by the best authors!

MIRANDA LEE

"...another scandalously sensual winner"
—*Romantic Times*

&

LYNNE GRAHAM

"(Her) strong-willed, hard-loving characters are the sensual
stuff dreams are made of"—*Romantic Times*

Look out next month for:

MISTRESS OF DECEPTION by Miranda Lee
Harlequin Presents #1791

CRIME OF PASSION by Lynne Graham
Harlequin Presents #1792

Harlequin Presents—the best has just gotten better!
Available in February wherever Harlequin books are sold.